FAR AND WIDE

Stories from the

Michael Round Prize 2025

Croydon Writers

Copyright © 2025 the writers of individual stories.
Other sections are copyright © 2025 Croydon Writers

The right of the individual writers to be identified as the author of this work has been asserted in accordance with sections 77 and 78 of the Copyright Designs and Patents Act 1988

All rights reserved

The characters and events portrayed in this book are fictitious. Any similarity to real persons, living or dead, is coincidental and not intended by the author.

No part of this book may be reproduced, or stored in a retrieval system, or transmitted in any form or by any means, electronic, mechanical, photocopying, recording, or otherwise, without express written permission of the copyright owner.

ISBN:9798271388989

Cover design by Jo Bodley. The Pomegranate motif is from the Palestinian embroidery tradition of *tatreez*, mentioned in the winning story

CONTENTS

Introduction 1
First Place 5
We Only Had One Religion 6
Second Place 11
Sniggery Wood 12
Shortlisted Stories 18
Missing 19
Why Don't You Just Keep Going 26
Dust to Dust 33
The Distance Between Postcards 42
From the Land of Beautiful Horses 47
Far and Wide 51
Alec Investigates: 55
The Gathering 61
The Frontier Keeper 66
A Frame in Time 73
The Secret Passenger 79
Beneath the Crimson Sky 82
Far and Wide 87
Far and Wide 93
A Happy Niche in Camden Town 97
Adelasia 100

Finding Sanctuary 106
Homing 112
Night Visitor 116
Nobody 122
Our Day Trip into the Sixth Dimension
.... 128
Three Odd Travellers 135
The Last Voyage 140
As Far Away As This 144
The Diary 151
What Lies Within 158
The Great Escape 165
Shay Goodbye 168
The Road To Nowhere 172
What Might Unfold 179
Mira's world 185
32 kilometres 189
Rider Of The Wild Ocean Winds 195
You Ain't Never Had a Freak Like Me
.... 201
About Croydon Writers 209

Far and Wide

Introduction

2025 was a notable year for Croydon Writers. It marked eighty years since our foundation, and less happily it was the first year since the passing of our much-missed Chair Michael Round in the preceding July.

After a life of military and teaching service, Michael became an invaluable mentor to many local writers. He published some of their books as well as his own, the latest of which, entitled *Genius*, came out just before he passed away. His energy and example were the power that drove our writing group forward, and he has been badly missed.

A writing contest named in his honour seemed a most fitting tribute, and older members reminded us that Croydon Writers had run competitions in earlier years. An open international one in the era of email and internet was of course a new challenge: but we pulled it off and I think Michael would have been pleased.

Gratifyingly, the competition was popular, attracting more than 270 entries from 37 different countries, with about half coming from the United Kingdom. The ultimate winner was Hashmi-al-Haseeb Faisal from Pakistan with the story 'We

Only Had One Religion'. The standard of writing was high and I know the judges found their task challenging. Unfortunately some very good stories were put out of the running by the lack of a strong connection with the theme of the competition. I'm glad to say that we have been able to include a few of these in this anthology, which offers a selection of just some of the stories we enjoyed. We hope none of those whose work could not be included will feel discouraged.

We hope in future to do more publishing, run more competitions, and expand our activities both online and in real life. Please check out our website at https://croydonwriters.co.uk/ and if you are within reach of Croydon, come along to our regular meetings.

Happy reading!

Peter Hankins (Editor)

Croydon Writers

Far and Wide

Dedicated to the memory of our late Chairman

Michael Round

15 September 1937 – 6 July 2024

Far and Wide

Far and Wide

First Place

The overall winner of our competition

Far and Wide

We Only Had One Religion

Hashmi-al-Haseeb Faisal

Hashmi-al-Haseeb Faisal is a Pakistani poet and multi-disciplinary artist of Arab-Persian descent, born and raised in Multan—a city renowned for its Sufi heritage. He writes in both English and Urdu, blending archaic diction, classical imagery, and philosophical depth with contemporary themes. A student of Human Nutrition and Dietetics in Bahauddin Zakariya University, he has won more than 25 national literary competitions. His influences include Iqbal, Ghalib, Tennyson, and Eliot.

***

'Twas I, mine own self, who did contend within, then wept beneath the waning light of eventide. My gaze lay askance to the dusken'd horizon, watching the sun slowly descend, bearing away sundry shadows of my soul and the frail hope once gleaned in an orphanage. Sweetness was but an elusive phantasm, akin to a moth drawn forth to flame, fair in vision but fatal in truth. Now remained naught but errant echoes of a bygone solace and crumbled episodes of memory.

Far and Wide

How soft the evening grew after that as though the air, dense with old sorrows, had grown weary of its own mourning. A strange hush, not of peace but of pause, drifted down. I knelt, fingers trailing ash, the wind folding round my shoulders like my foster mother's tatreez shawl, long vanished now, that indigo weave embroidered with thread as red as sumac, the pattern like falling pomegranate seeds. I remembered how she'd hum a lullaby, always a little off-key, when stitching and I, a child, would pretend not to listen, though I knew the song better than my own name.

Then came scent, faint and unbidden, of cardamom and olive smoke as if some memory had taken root in the land itself, blossoming ghostlike through the wreckage. That land— how it held things and how it remembered, beneath every stone, a name and beneath every tree, a voice. Even the olives, still clinging to charred branches, seemed to whisper of ancestors who had sung while planting them.

Somewhere, a kettle whistled, not in my world but in the memory of a world, perhaps my grandmother's. A hand reached to pour qahwa that would never be drunk and in the silence that followed, I almost heard the clinking of small glasses on a brass tray.

I walked on. Not forward, not back. The path turned inward.

Far and Wide

At length, through the wavering heat, I glimpsed it: Al-Aqsa's dome, golden as a fig at dusk, cradled in the arms of a city too ancient to break and in that moment, it seemed even stone could feel, could grieve, could endure and could pray.

There were fig and olive trees too, though fewer now, their branches knotted like old fingers in prayer. Beneath one, I sat, not seeking shade but something else, a presence, perhaps a remembering. Dust clung to my calves and ants carried away grains of sand as if they were rearranging history itself. The silence pressed in. Then, faintly, footsteps. No, heartbeats! No, drums!

Dabke!

Not the music, not the real thing but the echo of it, rhythmic, rooted and rebellious, rose through the soles of my feet and stirred the blood. I recalled the time cousins danced on it at a wedding in the courtyard, their heels striking earth with joy, with defiance. I had clapped along, uncertain, too young to understand the weight of celebration in a world where laughter must hide.

Now, no music. Only memory but memory sufficed.

In that moment, I thought I understood that what is taken in fire returns in seed. Our dead are not vanished but scattered like olive pits flung into soil, awaiting their season.

Far and Wide

I looked again toward the city. Its stones were still weeping but they were singing too and somewhere, carried on the sea-wind from Gaza's broken coast, came the scent of fresh musakhan—sumac, onions, oil—rising like incense from kitchens that refused to forget how to feed the living.

Then, I espied a bird, dying, yet striving for its kin. Therein I saw: a foster-mother's touch deeper than skin. My homestead was burnt in the balefire of genocide. Yet from the ashes, plume sketched a wraith, a shadow who left swaddling cloth at the burnt door.

Despair hovered but never wholly took root. Even in ruin, some rooms refuse to close. I was born orphan but never homeless. The orphanage had fallen to ash, the door blackened yet still, unknown hands laid infants there, wrapped in rags and silence. Their bodies were like plastic bags, capable of feeling, yet weightless, tossed by fate. Their lives were no sturdier than vagrant sacks of oiled cloth, light as chaff, yet brimmed with mute sentience, subject to the whims of wind and will.

I had to survive, not for myself but for them. I had to continue what the burnt door began, the legacy of my orphanage. Pessimism was not an option.

We, the children of that door, knew no creed but kindness. We prayed in different tongues yet to the same God, the One of Abraham, of Moses, of Jesus,

Far and Wide

of Muhammad, peace be upon them all. There were no enemies in our dormitory. The Qur'an and the Bible shared our shelf. Neither did we bow to idols. We had only one religion: humanity.

It is not scripture that teaches hate, it is men. It is not faith that spills blood, it is power dressed in holy robes. Those who murder mothers are not martyrs. Those who silence children are not soldiers of God. Those who desire to extend the boundaries of their nation are political leaders, not civilians. The victims are neither Muslims alone nor Jews alone, they are sons, daughters, bread-bakers and lullaby-singers.

I, the orphan, say that hatred will not free us. It will only bury our stories beneath another generation of stone.

Far and Wide

Second Place

Our Runner Up

Far and Wide

Sniggery Wood

Stuart Wilks-Heeg

Stuart Wilks-Heeg has recently begun writing fiction. In his other life, he is a Professor of Politics at the University of Liverpool. He lives in Crosby, Merseyside and, from 2023-25, he was the stadium announcer for Marine Football Club.

***

The red arrow on Cathy's phone told her she was moving from one grid square to another.

She was certain she shouldn't be on this golf course, but it was deserted and nobody was likely to challenge her. Golf was banned under current Covid restrictions and heavy rain meant there was little chance of anyone else being around today.

Taking refuge in a small hut just off the fairway, Cathy sipped the warm coffee she'd brought in a flask. She added some notes on her phone about the grid square she'd just left and took an initial photo of the one she'd just entered. Given today's progress, updating her blog with entries for eight grid squares that evening was realistic.

Far and Wide

The blog was Cathy's lockdown project, her response to how the pandemic had shrunk her world. She hadn't left her neighbourhood for months, her asthma making her even more cautious than most people in their 50s. If it hadn't been for the news of Susan's death, there was no way she'd be doing this. She wasn't one for hiking, couldn't read a compass and hadn't touched an Ordinance Survey map since the one she'd pored over with Susan as childhood friends.

Thankfully, OS Explorer Map 285, which included the road she lived in, came with an access code to view the map on a phone. Even then, Cathy didn't think of the directions on her travels as north, east, south and west. Instead, she defined the territory above her home as 'far' and the land either side as 'wide'.

Cathy's blog would document what she found in every grid square on one side of the paper map, the physical world she had explored with Susan when they were in their mid-teens. She couldn't drive and was avoiding public transport during the pandemic, so she'd need to walk or cycle to reach the 360 grid squares on land (around 100 were in the sea, and she wasn't a sailor either).

The furthest flung ones would be a challenge, but her fitness was improving. She felt confident of making it to Formby tomorrow, a major milestone. Clocking up ten new grid squares should be possible, including four partially in the sea, providing she'd understood the tide times. The Formby dunes would also allow her to sprinkle her blog posts with the literary references she hoped would increase visits to her blog, which currently stood at zero.

The next day, Cathy cycled to Formby without difficulty. The wind had dropped and setting off early meant she avoided the legions of families who had begun walking the path during lockdowns, converging from far and wide to visit this stretch of coastline. Cathy was all too aware that Covid had rendered certain locations 'must-visit', word of them spreading virally online, faster than Covid itself.

Leaving the town, a rough track took her out towards the dunes. As the sand encroached and made cycling impossible, Cathy locked her bicycle to a signpost and searched her backpack for her face mask. She might need it if the dunes were busy and social distancing became hard to maintain.

The dune system was enormous. After climbing a vast mound of sand, Cathy took photographs of the area, the cranes at Seaforth docks in the distance. Twenty minutes later, she was sure she'd found a location from the novel. Cathy sat atop another dune, took the copy of *Harriet Said*, by Beryl Bainbridge, from her bag and leafed through to a page Susan had marked for her 40 years ago. Yes, this was it. Cathy added more notes to her phone, took further photographs and made a screenshot of the location on her digital OS map.

Within days, Cathy was proven right. Her posts linking the locations to the novel found an audience. Her social media promotion of the blog had been pitched just right. The dashboard captured a steep rise in traffic, with visitors originating from across the UK and beyond, or from 'far' and 'wide', as Cathy thought of it.

Subsequent posts followed the same formula. One introduced her readers to the shoreline of rubble by the Crosby Coastguard Station and detailed how the promenade was constructed from the ruins of houses bombed in the war. It didn't trouble her that some readers seemed more interested in the photograph of a stocking among the bricks on the beach. Once she'd built up the stamina to reach Southport, Cathy blogged about Christ Church, explaining that the original church had been consecrated by a future Archbishop of Canterbury in 1821. Each post generated a fresh surge of interest in her project, with Cathy now interacting with a growing online community about her highlighted locations, via social media and online discussion boards, using carefully-chosen pseudonyms.

After 46 days, Cathy concluded she could complete her project without visiting Ormskirk or Burscough. Online chatter about her blog was easily sufficient and was already prompting people to

Far and Wide

travel to remote locations featured on it. Cathy published her final post that Friday night, providing granular detail about a single grid square, surrounded by others she'd already documented. For loyal readers, reading between the lines wasn't necessary: an outdoor café, a path, woodland. Cathy checked her online accounts and retired to bed, ready for an early start the next day.

She approached Sniggery Wood just before sunrise. Dozens of cars already lined the grass verges on the nearby roads. Along the short route through the fields to the wood, men, women and children marched, carrying digging implements. The wood perplexed them at first. It was an exact rectangle, measuring 50x500m, surrounded by a ditch. They eventually found their way in via a small wooden bridge. Cathy knew the damage to the wood risked being substantial and that timing was everything.

After an hour, she decided her unwitting army had done enough. Dispersing them would be easy. She dialled 999 to report the mass breach of Covid regulations, the police cars arriving within minutes. Cathy watched from a safe distance through binoculars as the baffled officers

tried to establish what mix of Covid and criminal damage laws the gathering broke. She imagined their confusion as they learned that the crowd was trying to solve a copycat murder that had never been

Far and Wide

committed. Some of her nods to the 1954 Parker-Hulme murder case in New Zealand had been less than subtle but using it to lure a band of online detectives here had worked perfectly.

Waiting for the crowd to leave, Cathy studied the OS map in her hands. Susan had guided their adventures around this territory, their entire 'real' world, when they were fifteen, while they built a sprawling, parallel universe together in their imaginations.

In lockdown's emptiness, learning of Susan's death from Covid, memories of their alternate reality had come flooding back. Ideally, she'd be the one to now discover the time capsule Susan had buried, somewhere in the wood, containing their macabre teenage fantasies. But it didn't really matter – the fun, as then, was in orchestrating this event. All the material would emerge online anyway.

For now, Cathy would just wait until the police were called elsewhere.

She could always arrange that, if necessary.

Shortlisted Stories

The entries that made it to the final stage

Missing

Celia Gatward

Celia Gatward is a passionate writer who loves crafting worlds and bringing characters to life. With a professional background in marketing and media, she has always found time to immerse herself in storytelling. Her writing has been featured in The Swan Theatre's New Playwright Festival, and she has written three radio plays for Upstage Surrey Theatre Company, with another currently in production and a live stage play scheduled for 2026. Alongside her dramatic writing, Celia enjoys exploring short stories and poetry and continues to develop a children's novel that she hopes will one day find its way to publication.

***

This wasn't the first time, but something felt more definite. More real. Maybe that's how I feel every time he disappears, Maisy mused. But maybe this time....

This thought made the emotions collect in a ball and start to rumble through her whole body. This

Far and Wide

thought increased the beats in her chest and the pace of her walk.

This was not the first time Maisy, hands coated in a slick film, clutched the 'Missing' posters featuring the ever-adventurous Buttons. She had remembered the drawing pins this time, and with effort and some thumb pain, pushed the helpful tack into the wooden posts around her neighbourhood.

Not normally one for the glass being half-empty, Maisy's reflection of doom was linked to the fact that this neighbourhood was new. Buttons would be lost; he would be all alone. The previously familiar secret mossy alleys, quiet woodland paths and cat friendly hideaways were all now replaced with busy roads, alien buildings, loud sirens and an odd variety of aromas which could not quite be placed.

Although the traffic indicated otherwise, the pavements were soulless and the dark skies brought with it the feeling of the impending, as Maisy actively shook the cat kibble.

Not quite familiar with the surroundings herself, she tried to think like a cat, whatever that meant.

As she turned the next corner, Maisy could see that this street led to a dead end. Behind a detached house, which sat like a full stop, was a gathering of trees and what promised to be some sort of urban woodland.

Far and Wide

That's it, she felt encouraged, that's where Buttons will be. Up a tree, chasing a squirrel, playing in the branches. Yes, he will be there, she felt sure of it. With more of an optimistic step, Maisy walked with purpose towards the house.

As she approached, she noted that all the streetlamps were old fashioned and ornate. This was not what she had been becoming familiar with over the last month. The abrupt change from her country home was overwhelming and even the smallest details were an adjustment. To Maisy, everything now seemed hard, unforgiving and foreign. The buildings were without character, the offices were industrial, and the shops were uniform, with neon lights which looked like they would emit a steady noisy buzzing every time they were on. Even when the sun shone, it was harsh and unforgiving. The dappled lights that used to paint her legs as they dangled into bubbling streams seemed like but a dream.

Pausing for a moment, Maisy glanced around taking in more detail of this street, she was certain she had not been here before. It felt quite removed from where her small flat squashed itself. Hesitating, she wondered if Buttons really would have travelled this far. Would he have ventured into this unknown world with curiosity or fear? Why did this street feel displaced?

Far and Wide

Trying not to be distracted by her thoughts, Maisy continued hesitantly towards the woodlands regaining the purpose with gentle rhythmic shakes of the kibble box.

When she reached the end, she turned and glanced back. The streetlamps flickered, as If powered by candlelight and what struck Maisy was the fact that no other lights were on. Not a single one. Not a porchlight, a sensor light, no fleeting strip flickering through a curtain.

The rest of the street emitted no light. There was no sound either. There was a vibration of fast cars some way a way, but here, it was like she was in a state of suspended animation.

Maisy was robust, she had been through a lot. In fact, more than most. She had lost loves, lost possessions, lost hope. And although she didn't often feel it, she was brave, fluid and flexible.

Her only non-negotiable was Buttons. Buttons was her anchor; Buttons was her constant…well mostly.

The emotions were bubbling again, a wetness reached her eyes, and on this void of a pavement, Maisy let the tears slowly fall. The pain in her heart radiated. All the bottled emotions that were carefully locked away, surfaced. As though the process of searching had given them access to finding. The prick of fear that tapped at Maisy now was surrounding her every thought. Was she lost, what

Far and Wide

was this street, should she just turn back? The questions flowed again.

To the side of the house, a half-broken sign declared PUBLI FOOT. Brushing off the betrayal of her feelings, Maisy turned on her phone torch. Shining like a halo on a bramble filled path, which looked like the type of path you would only venture down in the middle of the day,certainly not on your own in the dark, with only a rattling box of kibble for protection.

But this is where Maisy's bravery can get her through but also it can overrule her common sense. To be fair, her bravery has often gotten her through danger, fear, overthinking and moments of unforeseen danger. For this Publi Foot was certainly unforeseen and to most, would be avoided.

Hearing a rustle had the opposite effect that it would on most people, Maisy walked forward with purpose again, ignoring the brambles as they attempted to slow her progress. She followed the winding path finding the appearance of a gentle glow ahead, Maisy could see that there was a wrought iron gate in-between a hand placed stone wall.

The detail was beautiful, made even more so by the soft lamp light which shone through a clearing in the trees. As Maisy went through the gate, she was taken in by how warm the air felt and how the still

Far and Wide

the trees were. It was the peace she had left behind. No longer could she hear the vibration of the roads. The constant noise that had bothered her for the last month was gone and tranquillity surrounded her.

She saw a lone figure seated on as simple log crafted bench and next to them, standing on all fours and exuberant in the chin scratches he was receiving, was Buttons.

The joy and intake of breath was simultaneous. There was no fear, no question, just joy and delight. He was here, he was safe, he was found. Their happy place, the woods, of course, her instinct was right.

'Oh Buttons! You found him!' Maisy approached with tears bubbling again.

'Of course, my dear, we have been waiting for you.' The figure replied. 'He would not leave without you.'

Although the words didn't make sense, they did. It was the release, it was the permission, it was the end of the search.

Maisy looked at the figure and connected to a soul who had loved her when she was small. A soul who she trusted and treasured until she was gone.

'Granny Lou?' Maisy questioned but answered with a hug.

Far and Wide

'Yes, my dear. Come sit with us a while, we have some time. We have all the time.'

Lifting Buttons onto her lap, Maisy sat down and held tightly onto her beloved adventurer. She felt no fear, no sadness, she just felt peace. A peace that was amplified by the continuous tone that had gently been sounding in her conscious, finally stopping.

Far and Wide

Why Don't You Just Keep Going

Benjamin Graham

Born in a former mining community in Durham, England, Ben's love of literature grew from reading the works of Joyce, Hemingway, Ginsberg and several other writers a teenage boy should really have no interest in reading.

After several years struggling to pay rent as a freelance journalist, Ben became a copywriter and editor in Edinburgh. He now divides his time between writing, reading, and frequenting the drinking establishments of renowned Edinburgh authors in the hope of finding some clue to their genius or, failing that, a good dram of whisky.

***

The first time my SatNav spoke to me – not to me as a machine converts ones and zeroes to speech to aid navigation, but really spoke to me as a dear friend might confide in you – I understandably assumed I'd gone crazy. You may be thinking, dear reader, that assumed is an overly forgiving term. Perhaps it was and I really had lost my marbles. But that is, to use the words of my digital driving companion, besides the point.

Far and Wide

I was passing the Golden Fleet Service Station just outside of Carlisle when she first went off-script.

'Why don't you just keep going?' she asked. I looked at the digital display. It showed I needed to take a U-Turn ahead, then turn off into the city and onwards to my next appointment. Despite the fact that Sandra, the name I chose for my sentient SatNav friend, didn't have a microphone, I asked it to repeat its instruction.

'Why don't you just keep going?'

#

To understand my reaction, perhaps I should tell you a little about me. My name is Lev Merchant and I'm a travelling salesman. At least I was. Office supplies, mostly. From paper to binders to printer ink, there's nothing I couldn't procure for the growing business. With no wife or children, I had nobody waiting for me. I spent half my life on the road, sleeping in beige-core motels and eating lunches in grey-ocean car parks. In short, there was very little tethering me to home; no anchoring body around which I orbited. Still, I spent my days circling the same stretches of motorway, the same lines on the map, the same constellations of service stations and drive-in motels.

So it was that when Sandra suggested I keep going, it felt like somebody had opened a door in my brain, hitherto assumed locked without a key.

Far and Wide

Perhaps it was the fact that I didn't have many conversations with women outside of talking about toner and staples, or perhaps it was her soft Irish accent – the voice setting I'd selected years earlier for its pleasing timbre – but something about her question lodged in my brain.

Whatever the reason, I did as Sandra asked. I kept driving. I circled Scotland in four days, sleeping in my car, or under a leopard body of stars. I turned south and travelled through ancient valleys, among hoary hedgerows and over primeval moors. I passed old stone castles and gleaming skyscrapers. I left London behind and gunned it ever southward, stopping only for my passport, before hurtling through the Channel Tunnel and bursting into the Continent like a wasp through an open window.

All the while, Sandra and I talked. But these discussions went beyond the typical, 'Left in 500 yards. Take the second exit on the roundabout, 200 yards. Continue on for 2,000 miles.' We talked about the world, about my life and about the lives lived outside my window in repeating but everchanging cycles, like young tides crashing onto ancient shores.

We debated the origin of stars, the true nature of the spirit, the agonising birth and life and death of civilisations. Perhaps the one subject we didn't touch on was myself. And onwards I pushed. After three months, I'd seen every inch of Europe's dusty

Far and Wide

piazzas, towering spires and flat fields. 'Perhaps,' I said, 'it's time I turned around.' But once you step off the path you assumed for so long was your only route through life, only to discover an infinite number of new paths, it's quite impossible to go back to the old way.

So I pressed on. I churned over indigo oceans, carved through thick jungle, crossed vast plateaus of dust and desolation. I drank vodka in Vladivostok, bourbon in Baton Rouge, mezcal in Michoacan.

It was at the top of the Andes that my car finally gave up the proverbial ghost. The engine, which I'd already had repaired several times, sputtered and barked before finally belching out a great burst of funereal steam.

Silence. I sat watching the snow curl in great whirls beyond the window. With the engine dead and the heating off, a great fizz gripped my skin and settled into my bones. The slow ripple soon swelled to a charge that rattled through my body and set my teeth chattering.

'Why did you make me drive all the way up here? Why did you make me leave England?' I cried to Sandra.

'I didn't make you do anything,' she replied.

'Yes, you did.'

Far and Wide

'I only asked a question.'

'But in answering that question, I'm stuck.'

'So you weren't stuck before?'

I scowled at the small rectangular device. It's hard to argue with an inanimate object, especially when it insists on speaking in metaphors.

'Why did I let you talk me into this?' I asked.

'Are you speaking to me, or yourself?'

'Never mind that. Where am I?'

'The point isn't where you are, it's that you went at all.'

'That sounds like bad advice wrapped up in a cliche,' I said.

'It probably is,' she demurred, 'but that's besides the point.'

'But now I'm stuck here, on top of some mountain in Argentina or Chile or godknowswhere.'

'The important thing is you did something, anything.'

I sighed and pulled my jacket tighter about me. It was true. I'd spent my life on autopilot. Ever since school I'd opted for the path of least resistance, the security of always knowing, even if that meant knowing nothing. For the first time ever, I'd chosen to do something. Still, the situation seemed dire. I had no idea how I was going to get back to civilisation, to heat, to safety. 'Let me ask you something, Sandra.'

'Of course,' she said.

'If the car is dead, how is it you're still able to speak?'

And just like that, she fell silent.

I hunkered down and fought the urge to sleep. Thick clouds of breath streamed forth from my chattering mouth. But she was right. At least I did something. If this was it, then at least I could go out happy.

I awoke to a knock on my window. It was a local farmer, bemused and intrigued at the sight of my little hatchback parked on the side of a mountain. He generously offered to tow me back down. When we reached the nearest village, I found a mechanic who agreed to repair the battered vehicle, although he asked several times if I was sure I wanted to spend money to fix something that was, by all accounts, a rusted heap of junk.

Two days later I was on the open road again. I switched Sandra on but, to my dismay, she offered only clear, concise directions. I drove down through Chile, all the way to Concepción and onto the vast coast. I gazed out over the grey-blue waters, the sunlight catching on the tips of the waves like diamonds embedded in subterranean rock.

'Please make a U-turn where possible,' Sandra urged in her clipped Irish brogue.

I smiled and unplugged the device. No more U-turns. What if, instead, we just keep going?

Dust to Dust

Katie Weatherford

Katie Weatherford is an actress, writer, and director. She has been telling stories since she was a child. In 2023, she wrote and directed an award-winning short film, "The Murder Party: Offering Unconventional Solutions to Heartbreak."

Katie is passionate about the art of creation and creating with kindness.

***

Have you ever met someone who you know was made from stardust? We all are. You know this, but this person has some true stardust in their veins. These people keep you in their orbit. They are magnetic. This is the kind of person Gemma was.

Far and Wide

I paused for a breath. No one warned me how hard this was going to be.

> *Gemma was truly made of stardust. She would hate that I am saying that, but it's true. She made you want to stick around. Everyone here knows this, so I'm not quite sure why I am saying it. In fact, I'm not sure why I'm up here at all.*

The ink smudged and ran beneath my pen. I was crying again, and I knew there was nothing else I could do today. I only had a few more days until the…. until I had to say this to other people.

I turned off my lamp and lay down. Sleep never came easy. How was I supposed to sum up a person into a few paragraphs? Especially her.

~

The next morning, I walked to the field where we would often go after work. It was just secluded enough, while still being open and beautiful. I sat

Far and Wide

down with my pen and paper. If I was going to write this anywhere it would be here. The sun peaked over the horizon and made me think of her. Everything did, but sunrise was her favorite part of any day. I think it had to do with the possibility in each day. This sunrise was more perfect than I could have ever imagined. I wished she could see it.

I opened my notebook to a new page.

Gemma loved the sunrise. Each day she would make sure to wake up just before it. She wanted to see the pinks splash across the sky. I think something in the rising made her trust the universe.

'You're making me sound like some poet or something.'

That voice made me stop in my tracks. I couldn't breathe. I looked over and perfectly, where she always sat, Gemma was reading over my shoulder.

Far and Wide

'Yes, I liked the sunrise, but I think you are overanalyzing it. A day has possibility whether the sun cooperates or not.'

'Gemma,' her name was barely a whisper. 'How are you here?'

Her eyes sparkled as she teased. 'What do you mean?' 'I mean…' The words were stolen from my lungs.

She was right there. I could touch her. 'I've missed you.'

'I have missed you too.' She wrapped arms around me. I had never felt anything so comforting. Tears brimmed in my eyes. She was real, solid.

'How am I supposed to do this, Gem?' I cried into her. 'You aren't here anymore, and everything is… wrong.'

'This is why I wanted to find you.' She pulled back from the hug. Keeping one hand on my arm, she used the other to wipe my tears. 'I want you to come with me.'

'Where?' I asked as she stood.

'Just follow me. You always ask so many questions.' She grabbed my hand.

I stood and followed. My mind was moving at a million miles an hour while she moved us further into the clearing than we have ever been. The sunrise was more vivid and beautiful than I had ever seen.

I looked at her. 'Gem, this is a dream. Right?'

'Yes.'

All I could do was follow her further and further. I focused on the feeling of her hand in mine. I had missed the slight swing of our hands when we walked. I hadn't even noticed it before, but I did now. She walked all the way to the edge of the clearing, the edge of our place. She tilted my face to look at the sky where the sun was no longer attempting to rise. It was full of stars. I didn't even notice the change until she showed me.

'I wanted to tell you, even though I am no longer in the form I once was. I am not gone. I am everywhere. I feel you tug at my soul when you laugh about our inside jokes, and every time you turn to tell me something.

'I am sorry I can't be by your side anymore, but I need you to know that I am still with you. I am a wave that has returned to the ocean, and this is the ocean.'

'I know, but how am I supposed to do this alone?' The tears that flowed down my face threatened to never stop.

Far and Wide

'You are not alone. I know you wish our paths together could have been longer, as do I, but waves are only special because they are fleeting.'

Gemma looked at me with such love that I knew I would feel it for the rest of time. 'Wherever you go, I'll be. This is the blessing we have as people. We got to know each other, and we got to change each other. I carry you with me, and you carry me with you.'

'I will never be the same.'

'What a joy to be irrevocably changed by love.' After a moment, she pulled me to the ground. 'Sit with me.'

We looked to the stars together. 'Did you mean what you wrote, when you said I was made with stardust?' She asked.

'Of course. I've always thought that.' I looked into the eyes I never thought I would see again. 'You will always be the most magical person I ever met.'

'If I am stardust, then I have seen the cosmos. You have seen it too.' Gemma said to me. I looked to the stars again and leaned into her. 'You've always known exactly what to say. They want me to speak at your funeral.'

'I know.'

Far and Wide

'I don't know how to sum you up. I don't think I can.'

'Then, don't. Just tell them I am happy. I am stardust again.' She smiled and put her head on my shoulder.

'I thought you were a wave.' I laughed.

'If the wave can return to the ocean the dust can return to the star.' She laughed with me.

That sound.

'I suppose that's true.' After a moment, I felt the need to confess. 'I think… this grief has consumed every part of me.'

'Don't let it. You have so much life to live.'

'What do I do with the love that I still have for you?'

'Spread it. Please let others feel it.'

Another tear fell as I leaned further in, 'Please stay with me until I wake up.'

'Anything for you, my love.'

The silence between us was peaceful, as the stars began to fade into the morning sun once again.

~

Far and Wide

My eyes fluttered open, my cheeks wet with tears. My notebook lay open on my lap; across the top, in Gemma's handwriting, it said, 'Far and wide, I will love you forever.'

Far and Wide

Selected Entries

A few more of our judges' favourite entries

The Distance Between Postcards

Andrew Blackman

When Mara hears the clatter of the letterbox, she knows what it means. In the stillness of this small cottage with its triple-glazed windows, her ears have become finely calibrated. She knows the thud of the newspaper, the splatter of plastic-wrapped junk mail, and the pregnant silence of a postcard fluttering to the floor. This is a postcard. This is Tomas.

The days when she rushed eagerly to fetch the mail have long gone. Now, she watches the steam rise from her cooling tea and stares beyond it to the slate-grey sea sloshing malevolently at the shoreline gabions. Tomas's monthly postcards used to bring him closer to her, but lately they've been reinforcing the distance between them.

When she can put it off no longer, Mara pushes herself up from her armchair and walks stiffly to the front door. Hard to believe that only a year ago she was still on her feet all day at a whiteboard, teaching Bleak House to wriggling children who would never see the value of the gift she was trying to give. Now,

Far and Wide

her body seems to have dried and hardened like the bladdery wrack strewn over the sea wall.

Latvia this month. She doesn't remember getting a card from Latvia before, but she probably has. After two decades crisscrossing the continent in that old truck of his, hauling denim jeans and garden gnomes and scented candles and video-game consoles from one end of Europe to another, Tomas must have sent postcards from every country at least once. She's been in this small seaside town for so long that she has no way of mooring these distant names and cityscapes, and they fly loose from her memory as soon as she adds each card to the top of the towering stack.

Mara struggles to focus on the messy, scrawled lines about a shipment of self-cleaning litter trays and a purple-hued sunset blossoming over a petrol station. Her mind is not in Latvia but in this seaside cottage, in happier times when it was full to bursting with laughter and shouting, breathless games and whispered secrets. To her parents and to the rest of town, they were known simply as 'the twins.'

If she could freeze her memories there, Tomas's monthly postcards would be a treat. Instead, they remind her of when those times ended: her parents' deaths one after the other, the ugly argument over the house. The money would set them free, Tomas said, but Mara had never wanted to be free: she wanted to stay in this house, where they grew up,

Far and Wide

where she could run her hands over the coffee table and feel the scars of childhood escapades as her parents' voices echoed off the cracking plasterwork.

Then, as it always does, her memory runs on to the terrible day when words were spoken that could not be unsaid or unremembered, and the only thing to do was to create a physical distance large enough to hold them. Tomas's postcards have always charted the distances in time and space (September 2025, Riga: 975 miles), and yet the long-ago words still wound.

So now, between the lines about sunsets and litter trays, Mara reads unspoken accusations. See how hard he has to work, still unloading crates of cargo at his age, breaking his back for pampered Latvian cats? No matter how far he travels, he is never free. In the early years, Mara used to read hope in those small spaces between Tomas's cramped handwriting, but that disappeared years ago. Now, they're just a compulsive reopening of old wounds, a steady drumbeat of loss and resentment.

As she reads to the bottom of the card, a line catches her eye. After some random observations about Polish forests and Lithuanian fast food comes a brief, throwaway line: 'Anyway, this might be my last trip for a while - Janey is ill and doesn't have much time left.'

Far and Wide

The card flutters to the carpet for the second time today. Mara gropes for her armchair and sinks into it, staring at the waves and gulping at the tea without noticing that it's gone cold. When she finally gets up and hobbles to her father's teak bureau, she glances out of the window and is surprised to see that the waves have already retreated from the gabions and are lapping more hesitantly against the eroded remnants of sand and pebble. She fumbles for paper and pen and writes the two words that have been eluding her for decades: 'Dear Tomas.'

A couple of weeks later, Mara waits by the weathered old oak on the corner. It never used to be the oak—it used to be just 'the tree', in the same way that they were 'the twins'. All it needed was a glance and a whisper: 'Meet you at the tree.' And they'd be gone, out of their parents' sight and free to say whatever they wanted or get into whatever trouble they craved. But Mara wasn't sure if Tomas would remember, so she told him to meet her by the oak tree at the far end of the high street, opposite the beach.

He's standing right in front of her before she sees him. It's only when he says her name that she connects this stooped, sallow man with the brother she knew. His voice is rougher, sandier, but still it's as familiar as the scarred wood of the coffee table. The years collapse, and she falls forward into an embrace to keep from falling.

Far and Wide

But as the physical distance collapses to zero, other distances remain. They pull apart, looking at the cracked, weathered faces that speak of all the experiences they accumulated in the years they spent on separate journeys, the experiences that now keep them so far apart that they don't know where to start.

'Janey couldn't make it,' he says quietly, looking over Mara's shoulder at the sea stretching to the horizon.

'I know. I'm sorry.'

They turn as one and walk to the beach, instinctively following the same path they did as children, in the same formation: Mara on the right, Tomas on the left and always a pace behind. All the people who used to call them 'the twins' have now died or left town, but their feet still remember the way and take them to the pile of old stones, perhaps a remnant of an ancient fort, mossy and overgrown but providing a perfect view out to sea.

'Where's the beach gone?' Tomas says.

'Same place as everything else, I suppose,' Mara replies, squinting sideways for a response that never comes.

They stand side by side, awed by the vastness of the ocean, each wondering where to begin knitting together the gaps and the distances.

Far and Wide

From the Land of Beautiful Horses

Christina Borg

I'd long thought about Cappadocia and those mysterious lofty cave dwellings carved into the rock. Who lived within their ancient walls of volcanic tuff. Katpatuka, the land of beautiful horses... As I tipped cigarette ash into a tray and drank my kafe metrio my spirit set to drift through puffs and rings of exhaled smoke. I saw my childhood all at once, and with such immediacy, such clarity. And I became a child again. I held my sated belly and laughed full heartedly as I remembered the freshwater well around which I played, turning its handle to lower and raise my small bucket, running, splashing about, five years old; the generous crackling heat of sunshine on my back, white peaked mountains, hills and streams. Our home. The soft tinkle of goat bells from nearby fields, the smell of thyme; chickens flapping their wings, clucking at their feed. The rooster's morning call. The tillers of the land we called our own. I heard the gentle tinkling of music that spoke to our ancestral past. Church bells ringing. I pictured icons before which we prayed. I hummed a tune close to my heart. A call to arms. My eyes moistened with tears.

After they received the order, many made a passage north through the Bosphorus strait, and by land with cart, donkey or mule. The donkeys flanked by their owners almost buckled under the weight of blankets, rugs, bric-a-brac, pots and pans, and bundles of branches for firewood fastened on each side of the animal with string or rope. Others crossed by passenger ship across the wide Aegean, noting its deepening shades of blue under moon and stars, as bright and mythic as an ancient Greek fable; a sea sometimes smooth as oil, and at times brutal, rising high and whipped up by strong gusts of aeolian wind. We caught the white crested salty waves as we took standing room on deck huddled together for warmth looking towards our new destination. I peered into the depths, delighting at the swift flurries of fish and blue dolphins swooping in and out. I studied the soft lapping of the water as the sea stilled. Mama cradled Despina in her arms, her cheeks sweet apple red. We couldn't take or carry much. Save the essentials, we were forced to leave behind most of our belongings. But we couldn't look back, not now. What would it serve? We'd been driven out.

'Goodbye, Delmisso,' I lamented and buried myself in the folds of mama's long brown dress.

Before we left Anatolie, Mama, a woman of noble birth, had the foresight to wrap five gold medallions into her thick belt made of cloth, which she pulled tightly around her waist several times. Each needed

Far and Wide

for a different point in our respective future, for life in the new land.

Our ship docked in Piraeus as fine daylight approached in shifting tonalities and layers of orange, mauve, white and yellow. People collected uniformly at the front to disembark as slow as the sun's rays warmed our bones after the thaw of cold night, and the cloudless blemish free sky turned powder blue.

After we stepped off, we set down our small trunks and baggage on the port front, and looked around with little idea of how and where we would live. We were not the only ones.

The daylight pierced.

I turned and watched as skilled boatmen pulled and wound thick ropes around iron bollards to secure their vessels.

At eight years old I was earning our keep, selling cold water in a terracotta amphora on the streets near the port. For a cent, I'd pour water into a tin cup, and offer it to a thirsty passerby, or to sailors and dockyard labourers. They were gracious recipients and drank from the cup as though they were taking communion. I earned enough each day to buy a loaf of bread to keep us from starving.

Far and Wide

In our one-roomed abode that sat on stilts above ground where mud ran and sloshed, we'd gather and talk of our patrida.

By seventeen I'd saved enough to see myself through night school, where I learnt mathematics and geometry. I was a dedicated student, and applied my knowledge to a trade that would eventually make me a self-made man.

Far and Wide

Maisie Dance

'When I'm grown, Grandma, I'm going to go far and wide. All around the world, and you are coming with me.'

'Well, it won't be for some time yet, David, and by then you won't want your Grandma tagging along.'
'Yes, I will, Grandma, you wait and see.'

The years went by. David finished school, went to university and got his degree. Then he went to see his Grandma. 'I'm taking a gap year, and I'm going to fulfil my dream of seeing the world. I'm going far and wide, and I'm taking you with me.'

She laughed. 'Look at me David, I've got swollen legs and bent fingers. I couldn't travel now. You will have to send me lots of postcards instead.'

When he got home, he told his mother what she had said. 'Oh Mum, I did want to take Grandma with me she always wanted to travel.'

'She's too old now, love. Why don't I set up FaceTime and then she can see where you are.'

'But she might not be able....'

'I will fetch her here. Don't worry. You just have to make sure the timings right.'

Far and Wide

There was silence, then his Mother said. 'And you can send her videos. Luckily, I bought her that

smartphone for Christmas, I will cook her a meal, and Grandma can eat the same as you.'

David clapped his hands. 'Yes! Thanks Mum.'

The night before he left on his travels, he came to see his Grandma. 'I'm still sorry I can't take you with me, but Mum has set up Facetime so when you go to hers, you will be able to see just where I am.'

Grandma shook her head' Just send me postcards and a message on my phone.'

David laughed as he waved goodbye. 'You'll be surprised Grandma, Very surprised!'

The next week she was indeed surprised as her daughter sat her in front of her laptop.

'Look at the screen, Mum.' And there was David, sitting in a restaurant. 'Hallo Grandma, I'm in Spain, in Barcelona. Here's my meal: seafood paella, and here's yours. Eat it up.'

There was the same meal that David was eating, 'Look Grandma, over there!

A flamenco dancer in a red frilled skirt came on the screen, swaying to the music. It really did feel as though she were there, sitting opposite David, watching the entertainment.

Far and Wide

This was the start of her adventure. What with videos on the phone, postcards and sometimes parcels. A flamenco doll and chocolates from Bruges and the once a week meal from David, wherever he was. In

Italy looking at the canal in Venice and eating pasta carbonara. There were so many places and so many

foods she had never had before that it became a blur. And best of all, there was David, smiling, After months of travelling around Europe, Grandma had a postcard showing Salzburg in Austria 'Sound of Music' country Grandma, More pictures when I come home. Have decided to leave the rest of the world until later. Miss you and Mum too much! Also longing for Mum's steak and kidney pudding,' Grandma smiled to herself. David had always been a homebody.

A few days later she had a phone call from her daughter 'The prodigal has returned, cooking his favourite meal. Will pick you up later.'

After looking at more pictures and eating a good old-fashioned English meal, David cleared his throat.' Grandma, Mum has arranged another treat. We are going on a little holiday, Guess where to?'

Grandma shook her head, 'We used to go to Eastbourne when your Grandad was alive.'

Far and Wide

He shook his head' I have been far and wide all around Europe. This time it isn't so far but (pause) wide- wide open in fact.'

'Wide open – but that's where ....?

'Yes.' Mum says it was where you were brought up, Grandma. A fitting end to our travels. Not so far but wide open.'

Far and Wide

Alec Investigates:

The Case of The Callaway Golfer

Ashwin Dave

Alec Dunlop, the British expatriate small animal clinician at Kabete Veterinary School, and Sam Samana, the Kenya CID supremo seconded to the Kenya Wildlife Services, were downing their Tusker beers as the sun dipped into the Naivasha horizon; a glorious 'wish you were here' postcard Kenyan sunset.

The pair, who had first met after a traumatic encounter with poachers on the plains of Laikipia, had become inseparable. Their joint venture in battling the ivory poachers had earned the duo Presidential commendations.

'Bwana Kissinger, your jeera chicken and the lamb kebabs were exquisite. Asante sana!' Alec had taken to the culinary masterpieces that Sam's Man Friday conjured up with unerring consistency.

Sam had inherited his housekeeper from the previous Goan owner when he bought the farm. The Goan, noticing the striking resemblance to the US Secretary of State, had nicknamed him 'Kissinger' and it had stuck ever since.

Far and Wide

The Friday night ritual was interrupted when Sam took a call from Muthaiga police station.

'Fancy joining me to help out the homicide squad? One of my friends needs help with the crime scene in Muthaiga – the forensic pathologist is already at the house.'

It took them well over an hour to reach Muthaiga. The askari, with the ubiquitous wad of miraa (khat) bunched up in the corner of his mouth, waved them through. The two growling Doberman Pinchers, tethered to the iron gates, promptly whimpered into silence at the askari's 'nyamaza kimya' (keep quiet) command.

Alec mouthed a silent 'Wow' at the sheer opulence of the immaculately landscaped gardens and the detached bungalow.

Sam, pre-empting Alec said, 'They run a bespoke safari company based at Wilson Airport. Tourists are flown directly to various game parks.'

Sam's friend, Inspector Rono, guided the pair into the study that also doubled as the front lounge – a large TV was on with the sound muted. The mahogany desk and the armchair bisected the room into two sections. The victim lay slumped in the leather armchair with his torso leaning onto the right. The dangling right hand, clutching a gun, partially rested on the floor.

Far and Wide

Alec, skirted around the desk, noted the pool of congealed blood on the beige carpet on the right. The vet had to stoop down slightly to be able to see the entry wound on the right temple. Rigor mortis had set in – the fingers still wrapped around the gun.

On the left of the enormous desk was one of those green indoor golf putting mats with a few golf balls scattered around it. A putter and a pitching wedge lay on the carpeted floor; a golf bag with the 'Callaway' brand emblazoned along the sides positioned nearby. Alec, with the practised eye of a keen golfer, counted nine clubs in all. Well short of the maximum 14 clubs allowed. He wondered where the other five missing clubs were.

Rono recounted Mrs Poole's tearful statement: She had arrived home after a shopping trip and as she let herself in, heard a gunshot. Dropping the groceries in the hallway, she rushed into the front room where she found her husband slumped in the armchair.

The hysterical Mrs Poole had told Rono that her husband was a recovering alcoholic and had been prescribed antidepressants. Their aviation and safari business had suffered huge losses over the last few tourist seasons. The downturn exacerbated by the repercussions of the 1994 Rwanda genocide. Tourism had slumped in East Africa and all along the Swahili coast.

'Where is Mrs Poole?' Alec queried as he examined the golf bag, paying close attention to the two clubs on the floor.

'In the dining room being comforted by Joyce, my constable. We quizzed the askari earlier – he had not heard anything at all until Mrs Poole screamed. The two Doberman Pinchers were by his side all along.'

'And the gunshot?' Sam questioned.

'The askari had dismissed it as a car back firing.' Rono offered nonchalantly.

'No other servants apart from the askari?'

'Mrs Poole had given the day off to the cook and the maid before leaving for the shops. Looks like suicide to me.' Rono ventured.

Alec looked at Sam and gestured towards the golf bag. Both sauntered closer to the golf bag as Rono looked on. He saw Alec and Sam in a whispered discussion. Before Rono could join them, bristling with indignation at being summarily excluded, he saw Sam kneel over and pick up a golf ball. Both men headed towards the kitchen. Rono followed them quickly, fearful of missing out on the discussion.

'Here, please have some water,' Alec proffered as he carried over a glass of water from the kitchen sink. Mrs Poole, red rimmed and still shaking, half

Far and Wide

turned and extended her right hand to take the glass. Her right hand, betraying a slight tremor. She quickly cupped the glass with both hands and took a sip.

'Do you play golf Mrs Poole? Is that your golf set?' Alec asked casually as he saw Sam enter the kitchen, his hands clasped behind his back.

'No. His bag, he was addicted to the game'. Mrs Poole, eyes downcast, barely audible.

As she took another sip and put the glass on the dining table, Alec quipped to Sam, 'Let me have a look at the golf ball.'

Sam, who was standing a few feet away from Mrs Poole and Alec, flicked the ball towards Alec, who ducked and side-stepped as Mrs Poole deftly caught the ball in her right hand. A split-second reflex action to stop the ball hitting her square in the face.

She remonstrated, eyes glaring.

'I'm so sorry Mrs Poole!' Sam exclaimed. 'The brand-new golf ball slipped out of my hand. My apologies.'

Alec looked at Sam and smiled wryly. Rono saw the fleeting exchange between the two.

'Bravo, Mrs Poole, smart reflexes. Thank you for your time and, once again, our sincere condolences.' Both retraced their way out, Rono trailing them.

Far and Wide

'Bwana Rono, hakuna suicide. Not a suicide, cold blooded murder.' Alec retorted as he got into the car. 'You might want to look into her background. She appears very much younger than Mr Poole. I didn't see a wedding ring on her ring finger?'

'To be fair to Rono,' Alec elaborated as they drove back, 'even Mrs Poole did not realise that the Callaway golf clubs were for a left-handed golfer. Fearful that the askari may barge in on her and in her haste to stage the suicide, she inadvertently, placed the murder weapon in Mr Poole's right hand. Had it been suicide, surely the gun would be in his left hand?'

'She could be ambidextrous, Sherlock?' Sam surmised.

'Even the ambidextrous have a dominant hand. Our gambit paid off with her reflex righthanded catch. I'd wager that she's righthanded, Dr Watson.'

As the Beetle snaked its way towards Naivasha, 'Sam, you had better call Rono and let him down gently – before the press splash his suicide theory all over the papers. Premeditated murder. Hakuna suicide.'

The Gathering

Jennifer Day

I didn't expect to see you here as we both clamber up the courage to share a piece of ourselves that would be stolen by one another that evening. That information was so personal it had been encrypted inside me, like a microchip on a device. I didn't want anyone to know about me, yet here I was divulging my guts up to utter strangers.

I notice a small moth flickering around the fluorescent light within the room as we prepare to share our lives; some of us anticipating this moment, some of us dreading the eagle-eyed others staring at us. In that moment, I wanted to be that moth free to roam wherever without having to acknowledge its existence or being to anyone. I guess some of us here had never shared a secret before; perhaps locked it away in a batch of butter full of dreams so no one could find it. I know this was me anyway. The thought of even opening up a little was a bit like a pandoras box to me. I was afraid of what was going to come out. I was afraid who would stay and how vulnerable I would be for the rest of my existence.

Looking around, I noticed a vast amount of people of different age variants. This was unnerving to me

Far and Wide

as I expected them to be bit more like me or rather let me say not dissimilar. By this I mean I did not expect the doctor, and I certainly didn't expect the solicitor or the grandma. I expected people of working class if at all. There I said it. Very judgmental I know. I then realized that I needed to broaden my horizons if I was to start attending these sessions. Surely anyone can come to something like this and not be like me. It was very narrow-minded, and I felt like an idiot – it seemed as though I'd been living under a rock with this ideology.

The distant sirens in the background become faint acquaintances of comfort for me. Background noise. This catapulted me out of the limelight a little.

It didn't matter that you were a doctor; it didn't matter that I was a laborer. It didn't matter that Sally was a carer, and George was a baker and Tim was a lecturer. What mattered was that we all came together to share something that would almost fill the other person up in a good way that an addiction couldn't and didn't.

The emptiness that echoed within the capacious room suddenly felt like it was melting away and a cool sense of shade waved over me.

I didn't need to feel embarrassed, no, I didn't need to feel shame. The glimpses of light kept peeking through the door as different people scurried in, late for the session.

Far and Wide

She then began introducing herself. 'Hello everyone, I'm Pam and I will be leading this session today, a very warm welcome to you...' Pam's voice trailed off as I began to panic about sharing about me. I had visions of wanting to run out of that door, but I didn't leave. Instead, I got used to the feeling of being uncomfortable.

I realized in this moment just how self-indulgent I was. All I could think about was myself.in reality, I guess most people are like this. It's funny as we are so concerned with what other people think about us when in fact people are just concerned about themselves. I still couldn't stop the nerves.

My hands felt clammy suddenly, I was nervous at the thought of speaking before I had even spoken. My heart was thumping out of my chest, and I felt as though I was going to be sick.

With immense trepidation, I uttered my name and explained how I was a recovering alcoholic.

A sense of relief fell over me as id said it. Heart beating in normal rhythmic sensation once again. Palms dry. I could now listen to everyone else's story without going over the same lines about mine in my head and spitting out a different version as the nerves ate me up in there.

When I listened to your story, I watched intently at the creases that drooped over your brow. You lived a hard few years, I could see it before you spoke, your face was tired, weary. The glum look on your face followed your whole demeanor and swept through your whole body like a taser. Your cheeks were hollow and your lips dry, loose... cracked. I found it hard to correlate the two. That you were a doctor, but you had a serious drug addiction that saw everything get taken away from you.

When you spoke, I swallowed hard. A lump forming in my throat and tears that had been frozen for years, I suddenly felt them forming and did not recognize this feeling; it felt alien to me. I allowed myself to engage with your pain, to soak up the atrocity of your addiction and grief. It was as if you needed someone to beat the grief out of you. To tell you it was okay to grieve and cry and feel that sadness that takes your breath away. I couldn't believe you had lost your wife and your two children which drove you to drugs. It was overwhelming as we shared parts of us, I could see the pain making its way out of you. Goodness knows how long you had been keeping that secret inside you for. The relief must have been worth it. We may have come from different backgrounds, different areas, been brought up differently but our paths in this moment had been lit the same to bring us all together on this evening.

Sally wasn't even from Denby, she had relocated due to issues with her coercive manipulating ex. Her breathing was stridulous, but she had mentioned it had been due to the overdose she had recently taken.

Far and Wide

The fact that we had all crossed paths was interesting to me. In any other format, a carer, a baker, a doctor, a lecturer (just to name a few) wouldn't all be meeting like this. Although we met in circumstances far away from our latter lives could have expected, that road is wide for all different people with addictions. Addictions chase anyone. My heart sank as I listened to the solicitor Julies story on abuse leading her to drugs. The emphasis on abuse and what that man did you to was just horrific. It helped me to see that not all of what we paint on our own canvas is the truth. What we depict and decipher is modulated into our own story and perception of someone else's truth. That hit the narrative hard. As we left the session, we said goodbye to one another and I felt a longing to see them again, yet I know far and wide these people have come. We will never see one another again.

The Frontier Keeper

Sue Diment

'Sir, we have arrived at our destination, the frontier,' the android said in its monotone.

For a moment, Richard was reminded of the announcements made at the mass transit station near his home, in California, back on Earth. Then he remembered. He had been in stasis, on 'The Alexian', a jointly funded Sino - American space mission to the furthest reaches of the galaxy.

'The frontier?' he repeated, trying to understand as memories flooded back to him. Richard manoeuvred himself out of the cylindrical unit and stood. Immediately, his vision blurred, and the ground swerved towards him. The droid caught him.

'A normal response. You will require physiotherapy and vigorous exercise to return your muscles to full strength,' the droid said.

'I see. Where are we? Do you have the co-ordinates?' Richard asked trying to change the subject. He had suddenly remembered that he was alone. There had been concerns that two or more stasis chambers would mean the ship wouldn't make

Far and Wide

it to the frontier before the power ran out. Hence he was the sole astronaut.

'Of course.' The droid brought him a view disc, with a chart on it. Richard could barely make anything out; the scale was so tiny. He stared at it, unwilling to accept the enormous distance across the different galaxies that were represented.

'The date?' he murmured.

'Approximately 2340 in earth years, which means that 94 earth years have passed since our journey began.'

Richard tried to work out how long he had been in space. Based on the speed of their craft, he knew that it must have been thousands of years, to cause so many earth years to have passed. Time became very complicated once you were travelling fast enough to distort it.

'That is approximately 22,652 of your earth years,' the droid pointed out.

Richard sat very still, staring at the stasis cylinder, failing miserably to grasp how long he'd been inside it. He looked up at the right view screen on the wall of the ship's bridge. Nothing but blackness. For a moment he thought it was switched off. The opposite view screen showed thousands of stars glinting lazily, reassuringly normal looking.

Far and Wide

'Is the right view screen malfunctioning?'

'No sir. Diagnostics show it is functioning normally. That is the border of normal space.'

Richard was confused. The mission had been to find the boundaries of space, the frontiers, if there were any. He just hadn't expected there to be nothing there.

'Our sensors detect nothing beyond this point sir.'

'Oh.' Richard looked at the chart again. He was having trouble accepting this. 'Nothing at all?'

'There has been a request that we identify ourselves. The occupant of the other craft won't speak to an android. Under protocol 301, I decided you should be revived.'

'Why didn't you say so before?' Richard wasn't sure if he was relieved or unnerved to find out this part of space wasn't completely empty.

'Protocol 476 states that a humanoid recently woken from stasis should not be subject to any unnecessary stress until judged sufficiently recovered to cope with it.'

Richard sighed. Perhaps this other craft was the key to it all. The forward viewscreen crackled into life.

Far and Wide

'Good morning. I am the frontier keeper. You have the distinction of being the first human visitor to reach the frontier.'

The viewscreen showed a small spherical craft, the front of which was translucent. It hovered at one end of a long cylindrical object that rolled lazily behind it. Some kind of space station? The far end disappeared into the inky emptiness of the frontier like a mountaintop hidden in thick mist. Inside the craft sat a creature with smooth green skin, and what looked like antennae. It had spoken in flawless English, with a west coast American accent.

'Your droid was kind enough to allow me access to your language files. I congratulate you; their simple structure was easy to comprehend.'

'Thank you.' Richard wondered if he was referring to the language or to the files. It had to be his imagination. This guy looked just like the Martian depictions in early twentieth century films! 'Ummm, greetings on behalf of Earth and er, humanity. My name is Richard. Do you have a name?' Richard asked, feeling he should try to remember all the alien diplomacy lessons he'd been given prior to the trip. It was all a bit distant, but it was coming back.

'I suppose, Harold might be as close as your primitive language will allow for,' the creature responded.

'Uh, well Harold, could you give me any information as to what, er, lies ahead of my ship on its current course?'

'I rather assumed you would know that if you'd come this far,' Harold's voice sounded guttural.

'You do know though?'

'Of course. It's my job to know - I'm the frontier keeper.' Harold smiled (well, Richard assumed it was meant to be a smile).

'So, what is on the other side?'

Harold's smooth skin crinkled around his antennae. 'My guidelines don't say anything about providing visitors with information - I just keep an antenna posted on the comings and goings. I don't think I should tell you if you don't know - I could be in breach of a security protocol.'

Richard sighed. He was the only human for billions of miles, and he managed to meet the only alien for billions of miles, and it wouldn't tell him anything because it might be in breach of a security protocol. Just typical. 'Well. I've come a very long way, and I'm not familiar with this part of space - couldn't you make an exception?' Richard stressed the last word slightly. The blackness ahead looked anything but friendly or welcoming.

Far and Wide

'Exception? If you're a first-time visitor, all the more important for me to obey the rules. Anyway, who travels this far without knowing where they are going?' Harold's voice had gone up a tone, and sounded shrill.

'But I could tell your superiors how helpful you'd been?'

'And presumably, you'll complain instead if I don't tell you? You can either go on or turn back. It's not like the options are complicated.'

Richard could have sworn Harold sounded grumpy, but perhaps they'd both been in space too long. 'Please will you provide me with some information about the, er, area ahead of my spacecraft.' Richard tried to sound authoritative.

'Please leave. This is a check point, not a space dock,' Harold replied.

Richard decided to move on. 'It will be my pleasure to leave.' He switched off the screen before Harold could reply.

Their craft slowly moved onward. Richard sat in silence, staring into the blackness ahead. After what seemed like hours, the craft emerged abruptly into the galaxy beyond. Thousands of stars glinted ahead. It looked remarkably similar to the one they had just left.

Far and Wide

'A visitor! I trust you have the correct access codes to be allowed to enter this part of space?' A familiar, shrill voice enquired.

The view screen showed a spherical craft with a smooth-skinned green creature with antennae sat in it. Richard looked up at it and sighed. Home suddenly seemed a very long, long way away.

A Frame in Time

Christian Emecheta

The cherry blossoms swayed around me as I hurried down the snaky paths of Ueno Park in Tokyo, trying not to spill my smoothie. Pink petals caught in my hair, and I couldn't help but smile at the families sprawled on tarps beneath the trees, celebrating Hanami with elaborate picnics and sake. Spring in Japan had a way of making everything feel magical and new—like the world was an oil painting someone had just finished, the colors still wet and blended at the edges.

But today, that magic felt different. Unsettled. Like the moment before a spring shower when the air grows thick with anticipation.

I checked my phone—still twenty minutes until I needed to meet my photography class at the temple. As a study-abroad student, I'd fallen in love with capturing the everyday scenery of Tokyo life through my lens. Today's assignment was to photograph "fleeting moments," and what could be more fleeting than cherry blossoms?

That's when I saw him.

Far and Wide

Standing under a massive cherry tree was Kai, adjusting settings on a professional-grade camera. My heart did a somersault in my chest. He wore a vintage Japanese baseball jersey, the Hanshin Tigers logo faded but still visible, and his dark hair had grown longer since December. Just like I remembered, he had that slight furrow between his brows when he concentrated.

Six months had passed since that winter morning when I'd fled from our photography club meeting, my chest heavy with unsaid words. The memory of our argument still stung: his invitation to join him documenting rural festivals across Japan for a year, my revelation about the prestigious internship waiting for me back in Canada, both of us too proud to find middle ground.

A gust of wind showered us both in pale pink petals, and I watched as Kai brushed them from his camera with familiar careful movements. Just like he used to dust snow from his lens during our winter shoots in Hokkaido. My fingers itched to capture this moment - him surrounded by falling blossoms, unaware of my presence - but I stayed frozen in place.

"Sumimasen," a gentle voice called out. An elderly Japanese woman gestured to Kai, holding up her smartphone. He nodded with that warm smile I knew so well, the one that made his eyes crinkle at the corners. As he helped her take a selfie with the

Far and Wide

cherry blossoms, I heard his light-hearted Japanese, mixing with her delighted laughter.

I could still remember the day he'd taught me to say "smile" in Japanese - "egao wo misete kudasai" - how we'd practiced pronunciation between fits of giggles until sunset turned the sky orange. Back then, everything had seemed possible. We were just two photography students who'd found each other in this vast city, sharing Conbini Onigiri and dreams in cheap restaurants.

My phone buzzed. A message from my soon-to-be boss in Canada: "Can't wait to have you join the team this summer! Your street photography portfolio is exactly what we need."

The notification below it was from our photography professor: "Class canceled, enjoy photographing Hanami on your own today!"

I watched as Kai thanked the elderly woman, then turned back to his viewfinder. The morning light caught his profile just so, and I felt that familiar ache in my chest. Should I call out to him? Wave? Or just let this moment pass like cherry blossoms in the wind?

A group of street musicians began setting up nearby—their traditional shamisen and flutes mixing with the modern thrum of the city. Their first notes floated through the air, a contemporary take on an old spring folk song. One musician wore a crown of

Far and Wide

artificial cherry blossoms, while another had decorated his flute with flowing pink ribbons.

My hands trembled as I lifted my camera, not to photograph Kai, but to distract myself. Through the viewfinder, I spotted a young couple sharing Dango, their shoulders touching as they fed each other the sweet mochi balls. Click. A child chasing petal in the air, her yellow rainboots splashing through puddles from yesterday's rain. Click...

Then my lens caught something unexpected. In Kai's camera bag, peeking out from a side pocket, was a familiar lucky charm—the Omamori I'd bought him at Sensoji Temple during our first shrine visit together. He'd kept it all this time?

Drawing a deep breath, I opened Instagram. I hadn't looked at his profile since December, but his username was still etched in my memory. His latest post stopped me cold: a series showing the changing seasons across Japan, ending with this very cherry blossom scene. The caption read: "One journey ends, another begins. Last day shooting in Japan. Next stop: Canada's Cherry Blossom Festival. Sometimes life comes full circle."

Canada. My Canada.

Setting my latte down on a nearby bench, I raised my camera one more time. Not to hide behind it, but to do what we'd always done best—tell a story through images. I adjusted my settings just as he'd

Far and Wide

once taught me, and called out softly, "Kai-san. Egao wo misete kudasai."

He turned, startled, and for a moment, time suspended like a petal caught in a spring breeze. His eyes widened, then softened with charm. The corner of his mouth lifted in that half-smile I'd dreamed about for six months.

"Emy," he said, lowering his camera. "I was wondering if I'd ever see you again."

"You kept the Omamori," I said, gesturing to his camera bag.

He touched it gently. "Some luck charms are worth holding onto." Then he added, "Just like some dreams are worth chasing—even if they take you halfway around the world."

I stepped closer, cherry blossoms swirling around us like nature's confetti. "I saw your post. Canada?"

"Their photography museum offered me a residency. I thought..." He paused, running a hand through his hair. "I thought maybe this time, we could both chase our dreams in the same city."

The Shamisen players struck up a new melody—something hopeful and sweet that made my heart flutter. "I know this amazing ramen place in Toronto," I found myself saying. "They make their own noodles, just like here."

Far and Wide

"Sounds perfect." His smile widened. "But first—" He raised his camera, and I raised mine. Click. Click. Two perspectives of the same moment, just like always.

As we sat on a blue tarp under the cherry trees, sharing stories and convenience store Onigiri like no time had passed, I realized something: sometimes the bravest thing isn't running away to chase your dreams—it's letting your dreams change course just enough to include someone else's, someone that means the world to you.

Glossary
Hanami: flower viewing
Matcha: green tea powder
Sumimasen: excuse me/sorry
Egao wo misete kudasai: please smile
Conbini: convenience store
Onigiri: rice balls
Omamori: lucky charm
Sensoji: temple in Tokyo
Shamisen: traditional string instrument
Dango: sweet rice dumplings
-*san:* polite title after names (like Mr./Ms.)

The Secret Passenger

Tina Gillam

Standing at the threshold of danger, Amina's fear tightened its grip. Nearly all the money she had secretly hidden was now in the smuggler's hands, with the promise of escape tantalisingly close but riddled with uncertainty. Her overnight bag held only a few clothes and a small amount of cash; she'd left her passport behind, a calculated risk to mislead her husband. As she waited in the suffocating darkness of the safe house, the mingled stench of mould and stale sweat churned her stomach.

Amina's final decision to flee her abusive relationship had been agonising, a choice born out of desperation and fortitude. Now sitting on the cold, damp floor, hesitation loomed like a murky shadow casting its presence over her resolve. A sudden kick jolted her from her thoughts, a vivid reminder of the heartbeat she carried and why this had been the only choice. An oversized coat concealed the precious life that was growing inside her.

The door creaked, followed by a muffled whisper that seeped through the paper-thin walls, a signal that it was time to go. Amina followed the shadowy figures through the back door and into the night. The

Far and Wide

frosty air caught her rapid, shallow breaths, turning them into puffs of mist. Crashing waves, once distant, grew louder, each step drawing her deeper into the ocean's voice.

An inflated inner tube was thrust at her, making her flinch, followed by a rough shove against her back. The water slapped against her legs, its power undeniable, while the bitter taste of salt clung to her lips. The boat, absurdly overcrowded, tilted dangerously with every shift, threatening to capsize. She clung to the side and squeezed herself into one of the seats, her prayers drowned out by the chaos around her.

The smugglers then towed the boat out to deeper waters before cutting it loose, ensuring they were long gone if disaster struck. With the transaction now complete, the abandoned passengers were left alone to grapple with the merciless sea. The fragile vessel was tossed about on the heaving tide as water splashed over the sides, soaking Amina's clothes and numbing her skin with its icy touch. Time stretched endlessly, the moon a silent witness to the rising hysteria of the migrants.

The first signs of dawn brought the shoreline into view. The route had been treacherous, but this first glimpse of safety had solidified their resolve. Some cheered, others sobbed, but all felt an overwhelming sense of relief. Amina stayed silent. A single tear traced a line down her cheek, the only visible

Far and Wide

display of emotion. The baby she had so desperately wanted to save had remained still for the entire journey.

As she waded through the shallow water, she could feel the shingle crunching underfoot, and her body, worn and battered, gave way beneath the weight of exhaustion. It was too much. Amina collapsed on the pebbles, and as her eyes started to close, a fragile warmth spread across her belly...a tiny nudge from the life thriving within her.

Beneath the Crimson Sky

Md. Tanvir Hossain

Jean's twilight state shattered when flickers of blueish light danced before her eyes. Her senses slowly began to sharpen as she took a look around her. As far as her eyes could see was a never ending plain land covered in tall grass and brushwood. The land had a blueish glow while the sky was red. The blue of the land and the red of the sky blended to color the world in a blunt purple which somehow looked unsettling yet magical at the same time. A gentle breeze moved the tall grasses on the land side to side in a constant harmony. Jean realised she is sitting on a cliff, hundreds of feet above the plain land below. High enough to strike fear into a grown man's heart. But Jean felt no fear. No questions arose in her mind. Where was she even at? How did she get here?

She just stared at the endless land which looked like a sea, with waves of grasses and brushwoods instead of water. The red sky didn't attract her even in the slightest. She never really liked red.

Jean sat on the cliff and stared. She felt like the queen of this desolate land, sitting on her throne high above the ground. She felt undescribable peace

Far and Wide

and stillness flowing through her very existence and then again, the blueish light flickered in front of her eyes. It was not like the blunt bluish glow of the land, but a sharp, intense ray of light. Jean noticed it was coming from somewhere far far away, somewhere her eyes can't reach. Then just as suddenly as it appeared, it vanished.

Questions began to arise in Jean's mind. What was that light? Where did it come from? The peace and calmness she had felt moments ago were swept away, replaced by a wild surge of curiosity and greed. She wasn't staring at the endless plain fields anymore, her sight was set on the flickering blue light.

Jean leaped from the cliff toward the sea of grasses. From hundreds of feet above she fell, like a shooting star. She miraculously landed on her feet, unharmed. Not a single bone was crushed, not even a twinge of pain in her legs as though she were lighter than a feather. The blue light flickered again. Jean pinpointed its direction, but its origin was somewhere far far away. Beyond the horizon, unseeable to human eyes. She began walking, drawn towards the light like an insect lured by a lamp. She walked relentlessly for hours. After a while, she spotted some berries hanging from a random bush and scooped a handful into her pocket. They looked delicious and juicy. Yet Jean was so fixated on the

Far and Wide

blue light that she didn't eat a single one. She must reach the source of the strange light.

Jean walked and walked. How long had she been walking? Hours? Days? Months? She had no idea. Her legs started to ache, she felt washed out. She could hear her heart thumping loudly inside her chest. But the source of the blue light seemed closer than before. She couldn't give up now. She pressed in on her pursuit of the blue light.

Her mind was fixated on the target but her body started to give in. Her feet trembled, pain consumed her limbs, her vision grew blurry, she was hungry and thirsty beyond measure. Suddenly waves of crippling fear washed away the greed. How will she return to the cliff which she had left thousands of miles behind? She couldn't reach the blue light either. What was she going to do? Would she die alone in pain and agony on this barren land?

Jean fell to the ground on her knees, scared, exhausted. She begged God to send her back to the cliff. But alas! it was too late. Jean screamed, terrified as the world before her blacked out. Tears streamed down her face.

The hunger and thirst became unbearable. Suddenly she remembered the berries she had picked up along the way. She quickly reached out to her pocket and devoured the berries like a starved animal.

Far and Wide

The berries were as sweet as sugar and as juicy as ripe mangoes. It had a strong, almost hypnotizing aroma unlike anything Jean had ever tasted. All of her pain and agony vanished in an instance. She was no longer hungry or thirsty or tired—it was as though she had been given a new life.

Jean slowly stood up, took a long deep breath. She was no longer drawn to the blue light, nor the cliff. She sat on the soft grasses. The peace and harmony she had felt on the cliff returned. She closed her eyes and felt the mild breeze brush past her hair. She thanked God for letting her live, for the delicious, heavenly berries that had saved her life.

"Jean! Jean!!" Suddenly a distant shout cut into her ears. The voice was very familiar, but Jean couldn't recognize it. The shouts quickly became louder and clearer, as if the owner of the voice were right next to her.

"Wake up! You'll miss the bus!"

Jean jumped up from her long, deep sleep. Her mother was standing over her with an angry face. She realised it was all just a dream.

Oh what a dream it was!

Jean wasn't thrilled about going to school. Her family had only shifted here last week. She hadn't made any friends yet, nor did she like the people. This was the third time they had moved in the last couple of months. Jean's dad had been chasing a new career path which he believed would surely bring success and money. This was why he had left his old job and sold their old house. For the time being, he was doing a small job nearby.

Jean got out of her room and saw her dad in the dining room, eating breakfast. He looked exhausted. He had been losing sleep for weeks. Dark patches were forming under his eyes. Suddenly scenes from the dream flashed in front of her: lying on the endless barren land, exhausted, terrified, helpless. She saw her dad chasing the blue light from town to town while the true happiness—as sweet as those heavenly, delicious berries—was right around him: his family.

Jean made up her mind. She wouldn't be going to school that day. Instead she would have a long conversation with her parents

Far and Wide

Blessing Ime Inyang

Chapter One: The Restless Wanderer

Kelvin, full of energy, had always felt the silent pull of horizons beyond his village. While other children found comfort in routines, he carried a restless quest for something he could not name. His mother often warned, 'Your feet will take you far and wide, but remember a man in search of what he does not know may return more lost than when he began.'

He ignored her words. In his twenties, he left his village, leaving behind his village, his father's field where he was used to staying when he was disquiet. He took with him a small-crafted bag with a few coins, the strength of his youth, and a burning question in his soul. He wanted meaning, though he did not call it that then. All he knew was that there had to be something more than what his eyes were seeing, so he walked on, without looking back, until no one could see him.

Kelvin gradually walked past plains where grasses bent like the sea under the wind. He climbed mountains where snow meets face-to-face with the heavens. He then entered cities where the streets

Far and Wide

never slept and there he met and sat with sages whose names echoed in marketplaces and outstanding sectors in the world. Everywhere he went, he sought. But nothing he found stayed with him long enough to heal the ache in his chest.

Chapter Two: The Search for Wisdom

In an ancient city made with ancient walls, Kelvin became a student of philosophy. He listened to teachers whose names drew crowds, men who argued with eloquent tongues and mind-blowing logic. They spoke of virtue, destiny, and the order of the universe. Their debates stretched late into the night, and Kelvin was soaked in every word.

At first, his heart bubbled with hope. Perhaps here, in the polished halls of reason, he would find the unknown he had been searching for. He memorized maxims and wrote until his fingers hurt. Yet the more he learned, the hollower he became. Wisdom gave him language but not life. He could explain why the stars moved, yet his soul still wandered in the dark.

Kelvin couldn't hold it back anymore, he confessed this emptiness to one of his tutors, the old man only sighed and said, 'Meaning is a river no philosophy can fully expatiate. We catch drops, never the whole stream.' Perplexed, Kelvin left the city the next day

Chapter Three: The Pleasures of Men

Far and Wide

Kelvin turned next to pleasure. He said, "If wisdom could not satisfy, perhaps laughter, food, and companionship could." So, he surrounded himself with people, enough to fetch him what he is in search of. He feasted at tables overflowing with roasted meats and spiced wines. He grooved until dawn, music following him everywhere.

There, he met women with radiant faces and warm embraces. For a time, Kelvin thought he had found what he was missing. Pleasure blinded his restlessness for a moment; laughter quieted the emptiness in his heart. When the nights faded, and the revelry scattered, he found himself alone again. This time, the silence became heavier than before, and his heart whispered a cruel truth: borrowed joy fades when the owners are gone.

Chapter Four: The Summit of Mountains

Years passed; Kelvin's hair silvered. Yet, he was still going far and wide in search of something more. Pressing on, he heard whispers of monks who dwelled on mountain peaks. Kelvin, determined, set his face toward the mountains.

The climb was brutal. Ice bit his skin and the wind threatened to fling him from the cliffs. But at last, he reached the summit, where a small temple clung to the rock like a nest.

There he met an elder who had lived among the clouds for decades. Kelvin asked him the question he had carried all his life: 'What is the meaning of it all? Why is the soul hungry even when the body is filled?'

The elder smiled, as though he had been waiting for that question all along. 'You have searched far and wide,' he said, 'but you search as though meaning were a thing to be bought, trapped, or learned. No. It is not. You're looking for a destination, but meaning is not a place. It is a Presence.'

Kelvin did not understand. He left the mountain more confused than when he had begun.

Chapter Five: The Cry by the River

Weary and worn, Kelvin had wandered until his body could no longer carry him with the zeal of his youth. One evening, he sat by a riverbank, his bag empty and his heart heavy. The water flowed as it had always been since the beginning of time, indifferent to his journey. Stars appeared above him, scattered like fire across the dark.

It was there, in the stillness of that night, that the weight of his search pressed down upon him. He lifted his voice, raw and broken:

'Why does nothing satisfy? Why do I hunger though I feast? Why does my soul remain restless, though I have seen and touched all that men call worthy?'

Far and Wide

His words dissolved into the air, yet something stirred within him. Not an echo, not a thought born of his own mind, but a whisper deeper than sound: You have sought far and wide, but never upward. Meaning does not begin in the world you see it begins in the One who made it. You search for answers, but what you need is Me.'

The voice was not thunder, yet it shook him; not fire, yet it burned through his heart. In that moment, Kelvin remembered the old man's saying " meaning is not a place. It is a Presence. All his wandering, all his questions, all his hunger had been leading him here to the realization that true meaning was not in the scrolls of scholars, nor in fleeting pleasures, nor in lonely mountains. Meaning was a Person, and that Person had been all along.

Chapter Six: The Return Home

Kelvin wept by the river. For the first time in his long journey, he felt still. His feet, which had carried him across plains, mountains, and cities, finally rested. His heart, which had beaten against the bars of longing, found peace. He did not need to wander anymore. The One who fills the stars now filled his soul.

When he rose the next morning, he turned his steps heading home. His village awaited him not as a place of bars, but as the soil where he could now live with new eyes. He carried with him no bag of wisdom, no treasures of gold, but he carried something greater and bigger: The answer to his lifelong search.

Kelvin had traveled far and wide, only to discover that the end of his journey was also its beginning. The meaning of life was not found in places, people or things, but in the One who authored them all.

And as he was walking the road back to where it all began, Kelvin finally understood far and wide was never truly a search for things. It was, all the while, a search for a Person called God.

Far and Wide

Maroua Bensfia Khiyat

Manuel had never left the coast. The farthest he had travelled was a market town two hours inland, where the sea was only a memory in the wind. Yet his kitchen drawer was filled with colours from the other side of the world—postcards from his granddaughter, each stamped with suns, deserts, and birds he had never named. Every morning, he walked to the harbour and let the salt air bite his face. Boats came and went, men younger than him shouting about fish and weather. Manuel only watched, a folded card in his pocket, the ink already soft from his thumb. He had never seen the outback or the coral reefs, but through her words, he had travelled far and wide.

The cards began when Lucía left for Australia. At first, he thought she would return in a year, perhaps two. He told himself the distance was temporary, like a tide that ebbs and flows. But the cards kept arriving, month after month, each one a small window to another world. There was one of red deserts that shimmered like fire in the sun. Another of birds bright as jewels, perched on branches that seemed to glow. Sometimes she drew little arrows

Far and Wide

on the back, pointing to places on the horizon: Here I stood, abuelo. Here I thought of you.

Manuel stacked them carefully in the drawer beneath the cutlery. When the drawer jammed, he smiled and said the world was too heavy to close properly. The neighbours teased him.

'Manuel, you've never even been to Madrid,' they laughed. He would pat the drawer and shrug. 'Madrid is not the measure of distance. My sea reaches farther than any road.'

At night, he took the cards out, spreading them across the table like maps. He traced the outlines of mountains and coastlines with a finger bent by years of rope and salt. He whispered the names aloud—Sydney, Perth, Uluru—as though they were saints whose blessings could carry him beyond the horizon.

One winter, storms delayed the post, and Manuel grew restless. Each day he lingered by the harbour, scanning the postman's bag before it reached his door. When the card finally arrived, it showed a desert beneath a violet sky. On the back Lucía had written:

They say 'far and wide' when they talk about distances. But I think of you, abuelo. You taught me the sea is endless. Its voice changes, but it is always the same water.

Far and Wide

That night, Manuel dreamed he was at sea in a boat with no nets, no crew, no destination. The water stretched in every direction, but instead of fear he felt a calm so deep it shook him awake.

Years passed. Manuel's world grew smaller, his steps shorter, but his horizons expanded with each card. He carried one in his coat pocket even on days when he never left the house. Lucía wrote about her friends, her husband, the child she was expecting. Manuel's heart leapt at each word. One evening he sat on the seawall with a blank sheet of paper. He folded it into the shape of a postcard and wrote in clumsy English: I am with you, even when I am not. My horizon is where you stand. He slipped it into the drawer between two brightly coloured cards. He never posted it. It was enough that the words existed.

The final winter came softly. Manuel no longer went to the harbour; the stones of the pier were too cruel on his knees. He stayed close to the stove, the drawer of postcards within arm's reach.

In September, a letter arrived instead of a card. The handwriting was unfamiliar. Inside, Lucía's husband explained that their daughter, Elena, had been born strong and healthy.

'Lucía will write again soon,' he added. 'For now we send our love across the oceans.'

Manuel folded the letter carefully and placed it with the cards. He rested his hand on the drawer, as

Far and Wide

though steadying a boat in rough waters. That night, with the sea whispering beyond the shutters, he passed away in his sleep. Weeks later, another postcard arrived at the empty house. The neighbours, not knowing what else to do, slid it into the drawer.

The picture showed a coastline where cliffs fell into turquoise water. On the back, Lucía had written:

Abuelo, today I told my baby girl about you. I said you never travelled far, but you lived far and wide. One day, we will visit your sea. Until then, your horizon is safe in me.

And though Manuel could no longer hold it, the card rested among the others, a final wave from a world that had always reached his door.

Far and Wide

A Happy Niche in Camden Town

Miodrag Kojadinović

Sure, I am happy. This is one of the best cities to live in, in the whole world. Have a flat in Camden Town. Rented, of course. Dunno if I will buy. 'Twould be easier maybe. And cheaper once the mortgage is paid, but who'd give me a mortgage?

Yes, I make enough, indeed quite a bit, but it is not seen as a proper business here, so I present myself as 'entertainer' and 'assistant'. What I actually do is purvey joy and pleasure. Orgasms, if you will. Sometimes I get one too, if the john is sexy or if he plays the strings of the fantasy lyre in my brain expertly. I am not a machine, even though sometimes I must perform with machine-like precision and unfailing rendition. Everyone loves a bit of release, right?

It was a bit easier before the Brexit, but I had all the paperwork done in time and am a legal resident, even though not a citizen. As I said, I make good money and most of it is taxed. In our line of work you can squeeze some by and not report it. But I want to stay on the good terms with the HMRC. And by extension the Home Office. 'Cause you never know.

Far and Wide

I mean, they are OK. Nothing like the Securitatea my grandma was talking about all the time when I lived in Braşov. She was hung up on those s.o.b's alright. My mom not so much, barely ever mentioned them, and I saw my dad so infrequently it would have been silly to discuss the secret police from bygone days with him. He 'lived' just three streets down the road, but was mostly out doing gigs in Bucharest, or serving a sentence for fraud, and later started also travelling to the West to try to make money. Usually unsuccessfully. He actually inspired in me a desire to try London.

He didn't make it here and I wish I could tell him how I have, but he wouldn't understand. He would find it odd, and maybe outright disgusting that I whip the buttocks of men older than him for cash. The humiliations I dish out to those wrecks would perplex and upset him. He thought I was weak, on the verge of being a 'sissy', but he ascribed it to living with mom and gran, and was sure it would pass.

He told me so when I saw him last, at age 16. I came to London at 17, on a language school summer programme and then the law changed and we could just register we had a proof of residence and were no burden on the public funds. But to see me changed to the other side, and this buff from toiling at the gym for hours, day in, day out, when I don't have a client, dad probably couldn't relate to.

Far and Wide

Anyway, it does not really matter all that much. It is my niche, and London is a wonderful place for it. And family is OK when it works, not that it is always the case in my branch of work.

Ah well... prudishness. Tiresome.

But still, it's Europe, you should see what it's like in rural USA. Been there, done that, a client took me on a 10 day trip. Nah, not going back. Well, maybe to Hawai'i, sometime, but otherwise, Camden Town is my world, and indeed it is the world. Best of.

So there. Did you want to book a session? No? Next time? Sure, just call again. Thanks for your interest. Gonna scoot off now. Ta ta

Adelasia

Adam Lees

Two cloaked figures in black bandanas marauded the stony shore.

A piece of parchment hung on the dock, blowing in the sea breeze;

'WANTED FOR ACTS OF PIRACY'

The figures studied it, grinning.

'Just so happens that I've seen this dirty sea wolf bound for Cruz Bay.'

His eyes fixated on the island as it came into view, the jewelled horizon glistening behind him. He had lived at sea and he would likely die at sea but in his agonising search, he began to rue each wave. He had sailed the seven seas, climbed mountains and scoured endless crowds in his dogged search of her. Years had passed before he'd found someone who had seen her, his unwavering resolve pushed him on. He stood at the bow of the ship, gripping tightly on the rail, breathing silently behind cursed lips.

His sun-faded cotton blew carelessly in the sea air as he disembarked the galley. His stride was not careless, it was that of conviction, a long unfaltering

Far and Wide

conviction. The rotting gangplank trembled underfoot as he marched down the jetty through the crowds of village folk, they eyed him suspiciously. Maybe they had seen him before in years past, maybe they had heard stories of dangerous sea folk, 'gentlemen of fortune' they called themselves. From the shepherds to the smith's wife, we all knew they were no gentlemen. The fisherman and merchants of Cruz Bay parted to let the traveller through, his scabbard swinging conspicuously from his hip. Rope calloused hands pushed open the inn door brusquely, eyes turned on him, shadows whispered in dark corners.

The traveller approached the bar and produced a dusty parchment with a rough sketch of a beautiful mediterranean woman, scribed below read;

'For 15 years I have searched for Adelasia'

He then turned the paper to show another sketch, a wizened caribbean woman with wicked eyes;

'For 15 years I have hunted this witch'

'Alas, we don't see many women in this here fishing inn.' Said the innkeeper nervously. 'And we don't want you buccaneers in town neither.'

The traveller opened his mouth but nothing came out.

Far and Wide

'Call him what he is.' Came a cry from the back of the inn. 'He's a pirate!'

Again the traveller tried to speak.

'He can't speak, that's why he seeks the enchantress.' Said a soft, sultry voice in a foreign accent.

'A cursed pirate!!' Yelled the innkeep. 'Begone!'

He stared stone faced into the darkness as the figure emerged.

Lucious black curls framed her delicate olive features, she wore flowers in her hair and silver circlets chimed as she walked, silk flowing in her wake.

The pirate gasped a mute gasp and fell to his knees.

'I've looked far and wide for you, contemptible rogue.' She spat venomously.

He held her legs tightly, weeping silent tears.

'Rise, pirate.' She commanded.

He slowly rose to his feet, wiping his tears and composing himself. As his eyes met hers, she held his head in her hands and kissed him slowly, saying more than could have been said in all the lost years.

'Adelasia.' He exhaled in awe.

Far and Wide

'ADELASIA!' He yelled. 'I am free from that wretched curse. My Adelasia, I have never rested in my search for you.'

'You took too long.' She began laughing. 'Scurvy scoundrel, I am not the woman you once knew.'

The laugh grew louder, more wild, menacing, frightful.

Adelasia's eyes grew darker as her haunting laugh echoed through the inn.

The pirate stepped back in horror as her evil gaze pierced his soul.

Darkness filled the room and nothing could be heard except that insidious cackle. Silk turned to wool, silver melted and flowers died, left standing there with a wry smile, was the witch.

Filled with madness and fury, the pirate unsheathed his sword and lunged wildly.

He felt a sharp pull back, he could go no further, two cloaked figures had him by each arm.

The one on his left disarmed him as the one on his right punched him square in his temple. Dazed and confused, he was dragged onto the street, powerless.

A group of armed men in uniform came running along the dock.

Far and Wide

'By the powers, it's the law!' Said one of the men in black bandanas.

'What's all this commotion?' Asked a tall moustached man in a blue wool uniform.

'This man is wanted for piracy, there's a reward…'

'We'll decide the reward, thank you' Said the tall man, lowering a hand to his musket.

'We're due our reward!' Asserted the apprehender.

The tall man looked the cloaked figures up and down. 'You'll get what's coming to you, you can lay to that, gentlemen.'

Slowly, the shackled pirate's vision cleared as he regained his motor skills. He squinted his eyes and made out the wool hood of the witch skulking off along the dock.

He jolted to his feet, grabbing the musket and before they had a chance to react, he fired.

With a cry that echoed over the ocean, the sorceress was thrown off the dock, bloody wool flailing behind her.

Yelling, panic and confusion gripped the street. The law, the bystanders, the rogues and the pirate argued amongst one another as they bustled to the edge of the jetty.

He tried to scream but nothing came out.

Far and Wide

The body of Adelasia floated lifelessly, evil black eyes mocking him once more.

Finding Sanctuary

Michelle Lucey

The ocean stretched infinitely in all directions, a restless sheet of gold beneath the dying sun. Waves tossing the small boat as though testing her resilience. Salt stung her eyes, and her arms ached from gripping the oars, yet she could not look away. Beyond the horizon, a pale mist gathered, curling and humming, whispering promises she could not yet understand. Each heartbeat felt amplified, each wave a challenge, each gust of wind a question. She was far from home, far from safety.

Seagulls wheeled above, their lonely cries high-pitched, cutting through the rhythmic noise of the waves. The scent of salt and storm filled the air, tangling with the faint sweetness of distant flowers. She pressed on, measuring each oar stroke against the tide's slow rhythm. Shadows shifted beneath the water's surface, glimpses of shapes she dared not name, reminding her that the ocean was vast, alive, and watchful.

Hours slipped past. Memory and fear intertwined, recalling laughter and warmth she had left behind. Then, just as hope began to slip away, a shape emerged through the haze: an island, crowned with

Far and Wide

trees that glimmered faintly as though lit from within. Safe. Strange. Waiting.

She let the oars rest and allowed the tide to carry her the last few feet. Her heart thudded with cautious wonder as the mist thickened, curling around her boat like gentle fingers. The ocean seemed to sigh beneath her, guiding her forward, until her feet finally touched sand that shimmered like molten silver - soft and cool beneath her bare feet.

The trees whispered with leaves like spun glass, bending slightly as if bowing in greeting. Light pulsed faintly through their trunks, echoing her own heartbeat. Tiny, iridescent creatures flitted between shadows and leaves, their luminous eyes curious but unafraid. The air smelled sweet, of rain kissed grass, pungent flowers and wild herbs. She inhaled deeply, letting it fill her lungs, a balm for the fatigue and fear she had carried across the ocean.

She wandered barefoot over smooth stones warmed by an invisible sun. Each step was a threshold crossed; the fear of the waves and loneliness could not follow. Time felt different. Minutes stretched into a soft eternity, and the ache of hunger and thirst vanished, replaced by a quiet fullness in her chest. Nearby, a stream ran clear and sparkling, murmuring encouragement in a language she somehow recognised. Whilst not thirsty, she bent and drank; the coolness settled in her throat and

Far and Wide

arms, invigorating her in a way she had not felt in what seemed like a lifetime.

At the grove's centre lay a fallen tree, half-buried in moss that glimmered faintly. She approached it cautiously, drawn by the subtle pulse of light emanating from its core. As she touched the bark, a shiver ran through her, as though the island acknowledged her presence. Tiny creatures circled the fallen tree, their wings catching the light and scattering it in delicate prisms. They moved gracefully, weaving around one another in an intricate ballet, their soft hums mingling with the rustle of leaves.

The moss was soft and warm beneath her fingers. She traced the bark's patterns, noticing small depressions that seemed almost like writing in a language she could not understand. For a moment, she felt completely seen, yet not intruded upon; the island offered protection and curiosity in equal measure. She breathed slowly, sinking into the quiet, noticing the faint shimmer of spores floating in the air, like tiny stars suspended in sunlight. Around the tree, delicate flowers of every hue blossomed, some luminous, some translucent, their petals quivering as though breathing.

Night came slowly, draping the island in liquid indigo speckled with stars. Birds of impossible colours moved in arcs above her, their feathers catching glimmers of moonlight and mist. She found

Far and Wide

a hollow beneath a massive tree, lined with moss soft as velvet, and curled up. Sleep came easily, untroubled by dreams of waves or storms. For the first time in days, her breathing slowed, her heartbeat quietened, and she felt a fragile peace seep into her bones.

The island seemed to watch over her, the faint pulse of light from the fallen tree reaching even here. The hum of unseen creatures and the soft rustle of leaves formed a lullaby she instinctively understood. She felt herself part of the rhythm of the place, each pulse of light and whisper of wind resonating deep within her. Somewhere, the stream murmured over stones, gentle reassurance that she was safe, and even the vast, indifferent ocean had led her to this haven.

Dawn crept quietly across the horizon, soft golden light seeping through the mist. Sunlight painted the island in warm hues, making every leaf, blade of grass, and droplet of dew sparkle with life. She rose slowly, stretching stiff muscles and savouring the warmth on her skin. The grove's fruit trees bore luminescent berries that glowed brighter in the morning light. Dragonflies shimmered with intricate patterns across the pond, and petals quivered as though greeting the sun. Every step she took was accompanied by whispers of wind, soft ripples on water, and the hum of life that permeated the island.

Far and Wide

Tracing the shoreline, she found signs of past visitors: piles of stones arranged in delicate patterns, footprints that led nowhere, tiny boats moored and empty, bobbing gently. Others had come here before, perhaps lost or searching, like her. Some had stayed, some had returned to the wider world. The island accepted them all, neither judging nor questioning, simply existing as a refuge. A gentle breeze carried whispers she could not parse, as though the island itself remembered each traveller and preserved their stories in soft murmurs.

She sat at the water's edge, letting her fingers skim the surface. The ocean still stretched far beyond, endless and restless, but its pull no longer frightened her. Somewhere out there, someone might be searching for their own sanctuary. Somewhere out there, waves might scatter them, carry them, and perhaps lead them, as they had led her, to this place of quiet magic. She closed her eyes and listened — to the island, to the tide, to the soft whisper of leaves, to the pulse of light in the trees. Far and wide, the world waited, but here, for now, she was safe.

In that safety, she understood the first flicker of a truth she had always known but never felt: even the most vast and lonely seas could lead to harbour. Even the most wayward journeys could end somewhere enchanted, somewhere alive with quiet miracles. Somewhere she could finally rest, and

Far and Wide

finally belong. The horizon beyond still beckoned, full of unknowns, but she knew she could return to the waves when she was ready. For now, the island had found her, and she had found it — a sanctuary discovered after a journey far and wide.

She gazed out across the mist-veiled horizon that kept the island hidden from the world beyond. Then, faintly, she heard them - voices she thought she would never hear again, carried to her on a gentle breeze. Smiling, she turned back towards the island, and as the light caught her skin she shimmered softly — and was gone.

Homing

Kirsten MacQuarrie

'We'll win this war,' she tells Winston. 'Mark my words.' As a rule, Clem uses few, rationing her speech until less literally means more. Reverting to silence, she extends a finger to stroke her companion's cheek. Winston coos his appreciation, silver-tipped wings twitching with pleasure.

Trained to anticipate takeoff, he scales Clem's hand with shuffling steps, his pencil-thin toes looping lightly over her wrist. By now, Clem sees these spindly pink feet in her sleep, hazy reveries of human flight — no longer fantasy for some — blurred by bearing daily witness to nature's effortless expertise. In those early morning moments, down-soft and dreamy, Clem permits herself to nestle within that blissful, oxymoronic sensation of weightlessness grounded in great purpose. Would her colleagues stationed elsewhere along the relay understand? Even encoded, she deems it imprudent to enquire. Understandably sensitive to teasing, the Pigeon Policy Committee discourages whimsy in the strongest possible terms. It would not do to ruffle feathers.

Far and Wide

The dovecote at dusk feels serene, straw dust motes rhythmically dislodged from occupied pigeonholes to dance on air that tastes salted from the coastline below. On a still night like this, music and laughter alike carry up from the village, an impending blackout curfew no barrier to merriment that might entice some yet leaves Clement cold. Other young women seem to enjoy jostling for scant scatterings of fabric coupons or lash-fluttering over soldier sweethearts. Never her. She flies solo and always will. Her mother despaired, mortified by Clem's disinterest in and indeed impatience with children. Why must they squeal so? How dare they complain mathematics is dull? That failing precluded even a second-best destiny as spinster schoolmistress, despite the fine mind she could not and would not suppress. One day, after victory, will the world grasp that a woman alone need not be lonely? Battles fought against the odds are nothing new to Clem.

Grandpa Charlie was the sole one to understand her. A cobbler by trade; pigeon-fancier for fun. As a girl, Clem misinterpreted the term to suggest the pigeons themselves were fancy, or else her grandfather's labours of loving care rendered them so. Eager to champion his efforts, she hovered over the birds' silken crowns and plump, plume-rich breastbones, contemplating the best phrase — ideally, one word — with which to articulate each creature's perch on a colour spectrum running from

Far and Wide

pewter to steel and, on one thrilling occasion, white. Love stuck. It tends to. Soon, she knew birds better than most people and preferred them accordingly. Fancier in her own right, although Clement herself was never fancy. Charlie cherished her anyway.

'Trust your own compass, lass.' With one of Winston's ancestors cradled inside his calloused palms, the old man — or so he seemed; Clem wonders now if he was even fifty – had whispered encouragement into her tiny, attentive ears. Safe in that reassuring embrace, the pigeon remained motionless. Clem thinks she blinked. One heartbeat and all was still; with the next, some sleight of hand magic from her grandfather's skilful fingertips leased the bird back to the skies. Eyes screwed against the sun, young Clem watched, awe-struck, as it rose whilst receding with each elegant wingbeat; silhouette becoming a speck as it soared on a current she could neither see nor ever feel for herself. Far above, in every sense, a world that already weighed heavily upon her small shoulders.

A peck at her thumb, gentle yet emphatic, recalls adult Clem's attention to the task at hand.

'Sorry, boy.' Murmuring an apology the bird appears to accept with good grace, Clem supports Winston's splayed, scaly feet whilst affixing the correct canister, colour-coded to discreetly denote what Air Force bears a note for which ally. Minute metal leg braces, brackets delicate as clockwork cogs, secure her precious missive — here, too, brevity is beneficial — for the bird's mission. A voyage across, or technically over, the Channel. Winston never seemed smaller. Clem hears the Germans now employ hawks in response to Britain's avian victories: rumours of vicious interception passed anxiously along the nation's ciphered grapevine (or rather, pigeonline). A flash of sabre-sharp talons, of bloodied bones devoured in a feathered flurry of panic and pain, flits into her mind before she can catch it. Clem clutches Winston tighter until the poor bird starts to squirm.

'I'd rip them wing from limb,' she mutters, loosening her hold for the creature's comfort yet feeling her face twist into the taut, warping grimace she knows she shows whenever enraged. Mother scolded her for that too, each time her notoriously short temper struck as a child. Outrage at injustice always was Clem's powdered keg.

'Watch the wind doesn't change or you'll stay that way.' From a bird's eye view, she thinks there are worse ways for a woman to stay than angry.

'Blow away,' Clem urges the elements upon which Winston depends, deploying the full might of her mind to visualise her companion buoyed by a jet stream of energy to France and back in record time. Perhaps pigeons feel the same as she did growing up. Cooped up in cities, ignorant antagonists dismiss these birds as clumsy, ungainly vermin; heedless of

Far and Wide

the intellect and courage incubating beneath those admittedly unglamorous feathers. Their worth went wholly unrecognised until this war, Clement thinks as she and her comrade follow their familiar path to the cliff's edge. The same for some women. Especially women like her.

'Trust your compass.' She and Winston stand enringed by white chalk, water aglitter as the setting sun sinks. 'Then make it back to me.' Ruffling Clem's fingers as if giving his own wave farewell, Winston takes wing. Shrapnel-dull in shadow, his airborne body gleams streamlined, flowing like liquid silver through the last lingering beams of light. The bird's early, elevating wingbeats strike with cymbal clashes as his pace builds towards a crescendo but soon he coasts, strong span angled straight in resemblance to a salute. Clement returns it. She knows her home.

Night Visitor

Caroline McKenzie

'Come quick, shush, quiet!' said Dad. We ran, sliding along the linoleum floor to where he perched on the end of the sofa. He held back a frilled curtain and revealed the badger. A mystical and huge creature, experienced only on television until now. Badgers were a source of great fascination to us children. We could not have been more impressed had our father produced a golden eagle.

'You can give them peanuts,' said my younger sister in a too-loud whisper.

'Shhhhhh,' we replied in unison, adding to the noise. The badger halted and tilted his bicycle seat head, then continued unfazed. No doubt used to boisterous audiences appearing at the window. He moseyed around the darkened patio, snuffling for a while before disappearing into the woodland behind the caravan.

The nighttime discovery was all the more exciting for being called from our narrow beds, in the dark, and then slipping back under lumpy duvets, eyes shiny with the wonder of it all. The first childhood sighting of a badger is something to behold. In our nature-besotted family, it ranked somewhere

Far and Wide

between a godly intervention and a supernatural occurrence.

In the morning, there were silverfish on the bathroom floor and condensation on the windows. We climbed down the steps onto wet grass and watched mist roll across the campsite and come to a halt in a trap of clustered Douglas firs. The last wisps dispersed as the sun rose. We collected white badger hairs, the most valuable of treasures, outranking our pinecones and oddly shaped pebbles. Dad said he would make a shaving brush.

Blair Athol was our base, and we were mad about the village shop. It sold a marvellous, moreish thing called tablet, which came wrapped in greaseproof paper and melted in our mouths. Almost more astounding than the badger was the preservation of our teeth by the end of the week.

During the day, we would set off in the Cortina, driving through the contours of the prodigious Scottish hills. We visited Blair Castle, excited about suits of armour and swords. We were waylaid by the sight of deer in the grounds, trembling and unbearably beautiful. We watched in hushed awe. Later, we passed highland cattle, cartoonish and intimidating up close. Dad rolled the window down and casually said, 'Good afternoon,' sending us into gales of laughter in the backseat. The cows looked on stoically, their wide heads swaying gently, eyes fringed and shiny.

Far and Wide

We watched for the badger every night. We thought he was male because of his size. We artfully arranged peanuts, and he dutifully took them, not in the least grateful for our efforts, simply going about his business. Up close he had a long muzzle and teddy bear ears. His little eyes reminded me of a shrewd old lady; we didn't know his eyesight was poor.

Mum wanted to drive up to Arran to see the Sleeping Warrior. Dad said it was too far, and we'd have to turn around again by the time we got there. I wanted to see the warrior too, although I didn't know it was a rock formation and imagined more armour. Today, we would have looked him up on our phones; we'd have known everything without ever visiting, but you did things in real time back then. Had Dad known about the raptor population, we'd have no doubt found our way there regardless.

We went to Soldier's Leap, which had lots of history and lots of trees. Then to Faskally Forest, where we walked in the muted shadows of Scots Pine, calling out in turn as we spotted butterflies and mushrooms. Goldeneye ducks and a heron watched our progress along the way.

At night, we went to the clubhouse and walked back again full of lemonade and Tudor crisps, hushing the carrying voices of our tipsy parents. The river, which sealed off one side of the site, rushed past out of view but present enough to remind us it would sweep us away in a heartbeat. Frightening in a good way, like thunderstorms and balancing on the forbidden high wall at the back of the school yard.

We saw our badger eating peanuts on the veranda of another caravan, illuminated by the light from the window. He froze as we passed, but didn't leave, so we stood and watched him nose his way around while bats dipped above us, daring each other to swoop the closest. We retreated, each of us carrying a faint sense of injustice that the neighbouring caravan had somehow stolen him from us.

We saw Queen's View and were stunned by the long reach of the sparkling water, neighboured by green-cloaked forests, dense and unknowable. We thought the queen would pop up at any moment to see how we were enjoying her view. We people seemed tiny compared to the immense and ancient abyss. We were overwhelmed but couldn't find the words, 'Long way down that,' said the dads, unused to sharing their souls.

On our last night, Mum handed out hot chocolate and Trio biscuits. We were allowed to stay up late and hoped beyond hope to see the badger. We were so certain he would come and say goodbye. We were devastated when we didn't. The heartbreak of understanding he meant everything to us, and we meant nothing to him. In some ways, harder to overcome than those heartbreaks of the future, because nothing stings as much as unrequited love.

Driving home, sleepy in the car, we woke as the landscape flattened into the Northumbrian coastline. The enchanted Scottish forests and their inhabitants behind us, belonging to only themselves. Remembered for decades to come with the fondest of nostalgia. Legends of the holiday.

Nobody

Melanie Oliver-Trotter

Carol had never been to the states before. As she queued at arrivals she felt nervous. This was a big deal. Ahead, the man in the booth was working at the speed of congealed treacle. He kept looking at the couple in front of him , then their passports, scrutinizing every atom of their beings, until at last, reluctantly, he stamped their passports and moved on.

Carol reached down for her hand luggage, but before she could step forward a tall blonde had pushed her way through, almost knocking Carol over on the way. She wore a wide brimmed floppy hat, sunglasses and a vintage 60's Afghan coat. Her hands were encrusted with jewels and she trailed a short weedy man in a leather jumpsuit with a shaved head and a pronounced mince. She slammed the two passports down on the desk, tossed back her hair and preened herself.

'Get back in line ma'am, you're not next, ' the man in the booth said.

She jumped like she'd been stung, before pronouncing

Far and Wide

'Do you know who I am?' in a loud voice that reverberated around arrivals.

The man in the booth didn't blink. He looked straight past the blonde at Carol and beckoned her forward, saying to the blonde

'Step aside ma'am'.

Carol hesitated for a moment.

The blonde took off her sunglasses, swept off her floppy hat with a flourish and exclaimed

'Dada!' Like she was revealing something exceptional. When the man in the booth just stared at her nonplussed she announced

'I'm Serena Maddison, you know, from 'The Outsiders'. You'd have to search far and wide to find someone who doesn't know me. Just ask anyone. I'm a star!'

He looked unimpressed.

'I don't know that show ma'am. I don't watch reality TV, and even if I did it's not your turn.'

Serena was getting het up at this point. She was not accustomed to not being recognised. Back home in Omaha Nebraska she couldn't walk down the street without being badgered for autographs. She began to pout like a spoilt two year old as she shouted in the man's face,

Far and Wide

'But I'm a star, and I'm going to be a mega-star. I have been promised the lead in 'Seven Acres',' she waved the book she had been carrying tucked under her arm. 'You must have heard of that! It's a best seller world-wide. Everyone will know me once I play Emmeline! And when I meet C.J. Harvey he's bound to fall for me, everyone always does. His next book will be written just for me!'

'In the meantime, please step aside ma'am. These passengers have been queueing much longer than you and you're holding them up. Do I need to call security?'

Serena turned and looked Carol up and down, sneering like she was something she had just scraped off the sole of her pristine Manolo Blahniks,

'You want ME to step aside for HER! An old, ugly nobody!' She turned and flounced off, finding another line further up the hall where she could push and cajole her way to the front. Carol saw a couple let her in then ask for an autograph, only to be refused.

But meanwhile Carol's passport was stamped with an alacrity she didn't think the man in the booth possessed and she headed out in search of the driver who was picking her up, peering across a sea of cards until she saw the one that said her name.

Far and Wide

The next day Carol was in her meeting. Mike was really gung-ho about the deal. He'd flown over a couple of days early to work through the final details. But it was Carol who still wasn't sure. There were other options still on the table, less lucrative ones, but money wasn't everything. Max Warren was giving it the hard sell trying to convince her to sign. It was all about him, how successful he was, how well his films did, how he knew just the things to tweak to make it sell. He hadn't once mentioned that he liked the book, or even said that he'd read it.

He was interrupted by some kind of ruckus in the next room. Carol heard

'No, you can't go in there, he's in a meeting...' before the door flew open and Serena Maddison waltzed in like she owned the place.

'Max darling, ' she oozed, all fake affection and diamonds, 'I realised that if C.J. knew that I would be playing Emmeline it would surely swing the deal for you. I know you said it was our little secret, but I thought it would be such a lovely surprise.'

She didn't seem to notice Max's face turn puce. He looked as if he was about to explode. She slinked across to Mike and oozing charm and sexuality said

Far and Wide

'C.J darling! I'm SO pleased to meet you. I feel like I have known you intimately, ever since I first read 'Seven Acres'.'

Mike tried to say he wasn't C.J., he was her agent, but Serena wasn't listening,

'and I know Emmeline was just written for me. It's the part I was born to play!' she gushed, wrapping herself about Mike like a winter scarf on a cold day.

'I've got so many ideas what to do with the character, sex it up, make the film sell' she burbled on. But as she was talking straight into Mike's face ignoring the rest of the room Carol was standing up, suddenly certain.

'I am afraid this will not do!' she said, 'if Seven Acres were ever to be a film it will be true to the book. I will not have it spoiled for my readers.'

'Who the hell are you!' Serena exclaimed, the honeyed voice gone in a flash.

'Me? I am the old, ugly nobody who wrote this world-wide best-seller.' She said over her shoulder as she strode confidently out of the room. The last thing she saw as she left was Max collapsed in a chair being fanned by his assistants whilst Serena stood there, her mouth agape like a stunned mullet.

Far and Wide

The film came out three years later. It had been made by a small English production company and remained true to the original novel. It came with great critical acclaim and swept the board at the Oscars. Needless to say, Serena wasn't on the cast list, though of course she told everyone who'd listen that she'd turned it down.

Our Day Trip into the Sixth Dimension

Susan O'Neal

One minute we'd been waiting at the end of our garden, ready for our planned excursion, the next, a flickering mist appeared in front of us. Neil eyed it doubtfully, clutching our recently signed Travel Liability Waiver. He'd been reading the small print.

'Are we doing this or not?'

Not giving him time to answer, I pulled him into the middle of it. With a jerk that nearly knocked us off our feet, we stumbled into the Sixth Dimension.

A rotund figure bustled towards us.

'Safely through? My name is Tesco. This way please.' He turned and sped away.

'Did he say Tesco?' Neil panted, trying to keep up.

'I think so, sounded like it anyway.' I stopped suddenly. Neil cannoned into me.

'Where's our bag?'

'I thought you had it.'

'No, I gave it to you.'

Far and Wide

'Well, we can't go back for it now. I've got my wallet, we can buy-'

'This isn't your average day trip, Neil. Suppose our credit cards don't work here?'

'No time to discuss. Come on.' He grabbed my arm and we ran, following our guide down the passageway. I got a stitch and stopped.

'Don't lose him,' I gasped.

'Do my best.'

He disappeared round the corner. As his footsteps faded, someone cleared their throat and I whirled around. Tesco was standing behind me.

'How did you get here? You went that way-' I pointed down the corridor.

'Didn't Admin explain? Time and space work differently here. You weren't coming, so I slipped sideways to collect you.'

He grasped my shoulder and everything shivered - and then we were in a different room. Neil was stretched out on a couch in the corner, eyes shut.

'Neil! What happened?'

'Oh there you are.' He sat up. 'You missed the dinosaurs.'

'What? What are you talking about?'

Far and Wide

'The dinosaurs. We saw dozens. Great big ones, it was amazing.'

'But-'

I was bewildered. My normally sane husband was babbling, describing huge horny triceratops with beaks like parrots.

'Wait. Are you saying you've seen dinosaurs?'

'I've been telling you. Enormous things with horns on their heads-'

'Where was this?'

'A better question is 'when?' Mrs Stevens,' said Tesco. 'It was the Cretaceous period, a hundred million years ago. Now, you wanted to see Anne Boleyn? We must sort out suitable clothing for you. Can't have you at Henry's court in jeans. Come along. We need to get to fifteen thirty.'

I glanced at my watch. It was ten past two. My head was spinning. We went through double doors into the next room and I gaped at racks and racks of clothes. Velvets and furs and silks. Separate shelves for shoes and shawls, collars and hats, and wicker baskets brimming with underthings. The smell was overpowering and I wrinkled my nose. Body odour mingled with fustiness, overlaid with the smell of woodsmoke and herbs. Tesco offered me a dress of soft brown velvet.

Far and Wide

'This should fit you - I'll get Sipson to help you. This way.'

Emerging from behind a curtain later, I giggled when I spotted Neil. He had on a dark green doublet that fell to his knees but was split in front to reveal a huge codpiece.

'I know. Don't say it. Apparently it's the latest thing,' he said, embarrassed. 'You look

terrific.'

I felt terrific. My dress fell in graceful folds and Sipson had tied a small ruff at my neck, arranging a hood of gauzy material over my hair, before handing me a pair of embroidered leather gloves.

'What about shoes?'

She handed me some coral-pink silk slippers. They felt like cobwebs on my feet.

'Are you ready? Remember, you must avoid eye contact with absolutely everyone.

And silence is essential, your accent and vocabulary would betray you in an instant.

Understood?' Tesco shooed us out of the room like so many chickens.

We nodded. I was concentrating, trying not to trip over the hem of my gown while keeping the pumps on my feet.

Far and Wide

'One last thing Mrs Stevens. You do know how to curtsey?'

Well, of course I did. You just bob at the knees. I showed him.

'Oh dear me, no. You need to sink to the floor while lowering your head. Demonstrate please Sipson.'

Sipson deflated herself into a becoming puddle of sapphire silk and elongated her neck. I tried again and fell over backwards. The third attempt was better but my knees went off like starting pistols. Neil grinned. Tesco wasn't happy.

'You'll just have to keep to the back and hope no-one's watching you. Since Henry was thrown from his horse last month, and Anne miscarried a male child, his temper is highly unpredictable. Anything can send him into a vicious rage.'

'Sounds dangerous Liz. Are you sure you still want to do this?' Neil's eyelid was twitching.

I wasn't, not really, but I nodded.

'This way.'

Tesco reached for me and I felt the room shimmy. When the world stopped wobbling we were in Hampton Court's Great Hall, its vast hammer-beam roof arching over the spectacular space, with dozens of torches piercing the gloom around the walls.

Far and Wide

'Keep to the shadows and you should be safe. We'll see you later.' He melted into the crowd with Sipson.

Neil leaned towards me. 'You okay?'

'I could do with a pee.'

'You should have gone before we left.'

'I know. Ssh. What's happening?'

Dozens of courtiers were standing about, talking quietly. At some unseen signal, silence fell. Everyone stepped back as a small group came in. Ladies sank into graceful genuflections and gentlemen bowed low. I shuffled backwards and my shoe came off. I bent to replace it and bumped into someone, who rounded on me with a hissed oath. People craned to see the cause of the kerfuffle. As I straightened up, the crowd parted and I saw a vast figure lumbering towards me, face purple with rage. I registered a bulky bandage on one leg and fluttering feathers on his wide velvet hat before Neil grabbed my elbow.

His face was deathly pale.

'Run.'

We fled. Down a corridor, through room after room. Racing to stay ahead of the clattering feet behind us, I lost my other shoe, my ruff slid round under my ear and I noticed that Neil's codpiece had

Far and Wide

come loose and was flapping about with every stride. There was a narrow door in the last room and we slipped through, slamming it shut behind us.

'Can't go on,' I gasped, bent double. 'Where's Tesco when you need him?'

'Not obligated to help, if I read the Waiver correctly.'

'What?' My shriek was whispered.

'Well, Clause 13b was something about- in the event of a mishap, the Management was under no obligation to rescue-'

'Why didn't you say?'

'I was going to mention it, but you said 'Are we doing this or not?' and yanked me through.'

'So it's my fault, is it?'

Neil shrugged his shoulders.

Someone's fist hammered on the door. I felt sick. Summary execution seemed a high price to pay for not reading the small print.

Something touched my arm and I nearly fainted.

'Had enough? Like to go home for tea?'

I could have hugged Tesco, really I could.

Three Odd Travellers

Martha Patterson

One sunny afternoon Queen Elizabeth I, William Shakespeare, and his rival playwright Christopher Marlowe were traveling together. Shakespeare had proposed the trip on the occasion of his birthday, the 23rd of April. It was the late 1500s. They were traveling by coach and sea to Paris, where they'd entertain themselves eating croissants, drinking coffee, and speaking a language none of them spoke expertly. Queen Elizabeth I, with her shaved forehead and hip-enlarged skirts, listened to the others as she smoked opium from a pipe in their horse-drawn carriage.

'What's in a name?' asked Christopher suddenly. 'Didn't you write, William, that a rose by any other name would smell as sweet?'

'I did,' answered Shakespeare. 'My name is Welsh; it means having a purpose in life.'

'I hope we have purpose for this trip,' said the Queen. 'I'm not riff raff that can't afford to go anywhere, but I don't like voyages by water, and I'm mostly a homebody, happy with my court jester and the redecoration of my palace. I'm getting old.'

Far and Wide

'That's all good,' said Shakespeare, clearing his throat, 'but I subscribe to worldliness. I like foreign food, and seeing intrigues in which strangers from other lands engage.'

'I feel the same,' said Christopher Marlowe as their carriage lurched along a rocky lane. 'I went to the fancy wedding of my cousin in Spain. I loved the tarantella dancing and the bullfights. An engaging sport! As for my cousin's Spanish wedding, I didn't know what to get for a wedding gift, so I gave the couple two sheep and had them transported to Barcelona from England.'

'Livestock is always in demand,' said Shakespeare approvingly.

'My courtiers asked two years ago if I'd like cattle for my birthday,' said Queen Elizabeth, 'but I had a goat roast for the peasants instead - a reward in itself. Call me a stick-in-the-mud. I don't go out much anymore. I only met you two from being at your plays.'

'A treat,' answered Shakespeare.

'Yes,' said Christopher. 'My good Queen, when you saw Tamburlaine the Great I expected the royals to find my plot too full of bloodshed.'

'I loved it!' exclaimed Elizabeth.

Far and Wide

'Hold on,' said Shakespeare suddenly, 'we're passing a dangerous row of hedges!' Suddenly their coach tipped over like a house in a tornado, and the three of them lay scattered in the dirt. Their picnic basket spilled out, too. And at that moment, a highway robber approached them with a gun.

'Unhappy beasts!' he said. 'I want your jewels, your finery, and your sandwiches.'

'My word,' said the startled Shakespeare to the thief, 'I've written plays about the likes of you – a villain!'

The Queen addressed the robber. 'Good God, fellow! Do you know to whom you speak? I'm the Queen.'

'You may be the Empress of China for all I care. There's nothing in a title. Your jewels,' said the robber, holding out his greedy hands.

'Beggar!' shouted the Queen. 'I'd as soon give you my jewels as sheep from my lands!' And she covered the shiny things on the chest of her gown with her hand. But Christopher was alert.

'You picked the wrong subjects for your thievery,' said Christopher to the stranger, pulling out a pistol. He shot the robber, who collapsed dead on the ground.

Far and Wide

All the while the coachman knelt nervously repairing the wheel of the carriage. But then, cautiously, he inspected the robber's body, and said to Christopher, 'Now you've really done it!'

The three passengers moved more distant from the blood-spattered robber's body while they waited for the repaired carriage.

'He'll have a hard time getting into Heaven!' grunted the coachman, kneeling over his handiwork at the wheel of the vehicle. The wheel was soon fixed and the travelers were no longer in danger of spending the night in a field. The sun appeared from behind a cloud.

The coachman alighted into his seat, whipped the horses, and the three companions continued on to the coast, where they'd catch a boat and cross the English Channel.

'Justice prevailed,' said Christopher.

'Maybe I'll write a play about this,' said Shakespeare.

'Well, you're both experienced, I see,' said the Queen. She decided to give them each a jewel, and unpinned the stones from her bodice.

'I couldn't ask for a better escapade,' she said. 'And these jewels are in thanks for your friendship.'

Far and Wide

The two men were exhausted. They accepted the Queen's gifts, and continued their journey in unencumbered spirits.

The Last Voyage

Denarii Peters

Those are not oceans at all. No ozone filled waves to break and foam over solid rock; no islands wreathed in summer mist.

The sea is lost, perhaps more than a hundred miles away in any direction, and though great ships there may be, never again will I sail in them.

I could curse my fate, but where would be the justice in that? The path taken was my own.

My scornful laughter echoed from the rafters. 'Call them explorers? These men are fools and cowards.' A dramatic tearing up of maps. 'They can't be right. Leave it to me: I'll draw you up a set of new ones, better even than Magellan's. And wealth?' I spread my arms to encompass the room and all the riches on display. 'A ship and a crew are all I require to bring you ten times more than your treasury at present contains.'

The king was sceptical, his queen less so: I have always been a charmer.

'One ship?'

Far and Wide

'Aye, The Azure Ladrone would be my choice. And her crew are stalwart, more than eager for adventure.' These were the first true words I had spoken in so long, it was a surprise they left my tongue with such ease.

'You are at present her captain?' The king leant towards me; not a good look. The crown slipped a little on his foolish head.

'Yes, but not her owner. I would hesitate to take someone else's vessel into uncharted seas.'

Now, that was also close to the truth. The Azure Ladrone was at present berthed no more than a mile from where we stood. And I wasn't going to take her anywhere unless able to keep my command.

The chancellor coughed. 'Majesties, I would remind you the vessel's owner is being held in the cells, his ship having been seized for smuggling. This man is also complicit.'

I pursed my lips, shook my head a little and sighed, all the time making sure to hold the queen's eye.

'What say you?'

'I am innocent, Your Majesty. My crew and I had no idea what cargo we were carrying; the owner gave us no information.' Well, he couldn't, could

Far and Wide

he? Not when he was unaware the cargo had been switched for a different one while at sea.

They talked a while longer. But it was a done deal; you can always rely on greed to win any argument.

I left a few hours later as the owner, captain and master of my very own vessel: a much simpler solution and far safer than my original intention of seizing her out at sea.

Now my faithful crew and I had a head start. The king's ships would not be chasing us straight away. There would be quite a while before it dawned on anyone that the Ladrone was now a pirate ship. If indeed they ever did work it out at all.

The crew celebrated long into the night.

The king had provided money for a complete re-fit. Our ship would be fast, well-armed and well provisioned. I had a set of the latest maps. Yes, the same ones I had pretended to find amusing. We would sail into the newly discovered ocean and emerge to plunder anything that came near.

It could take years before anyone at home realised what was going on; losses are expected during dangerous voyages to unknown regions. By then we would be among the richest men in the world. Once

Far and Wide

enough wealth had been amassed, we could return if we wished or maybe settle in these new lands.

In the beginning, all went even better than I could have hoped. Our first victim was one of a group of three ships, but which had got separated from the other two. She was already in trouble, her crew on the verge of mutiny, driven mad by fear of falling over the edge of the world.

Her captain invited us aboard. But he didn't last long.

The mutineers, once reassured there was no intention to sail much further south, joined us. We used that ship to overcome the other two, again finding many recruits among the unhappy press-ganged men aboard.

And so it went on. Taking over a small island, we used one ship as spares for the others we had captured. Nothing stood in our way. I lost count of the vessels boarded, captains marooned, while those loyal to them were slaughtered.

I made only one mistake: I should have chosen a crew of honest men, not liars, mutineers and greedy cutthroats.

The day came when my own avarice was at last satisfied. 'Now, my fine crew, it is time to sail home.'

Far and Wide

But they did not agree; a truly greedy man can never have enough. Not even all the gold in the world can come close to slaking such an appetite.

There were arguments.

I ordered my sailors to obey.

Pretending contrition, they prepared to weigh anchor.

We celebrated our last night as pirates. I found the wine a little sour.

This morning, I wake on top of a mountain, too steep to descend without ropes. From its peak is only a view of dense forests and tiny, swift flowing streams. Above me arches a sky of the same deep blue as friendly waters. If I try hard enough, I can see the scattered clouds as the white horses of prancing waves.

But alas, I am only too aware that this is a high mountain. And those are not oceans at all.

As Far Away As This

Jo Riglar

When I moved to this city, I expected it would be an alien space. I knew that because I googled 'everyday life in Varanasi'. That first day I was discovering sights and noises and smells.

The peppery scent of betel leaves. The cows in the streets. The cow dung. The dogs and their litters curled up in dying embers. Near the Dewan Kulp Singh Hostel for Foreign Students where I'd rented a room overlooking the river, there were rotting animals dumped by the roadside stalls.

I had to get as far away from you as this.

My first night was new. New bed empty of you. New money spent alone. New smells not of your body.

I had two days before I was to report at The Sanskruti International School. My new exciting job. A new realisation of me. My empowerment.

Their advert was odd. They were looking for high precision individuals, 'just like me'. I decided it was a mistranslation. I had lots of experience, was used to responsibility. It should really be a 'walk in the park' as my 'assigned colleague' had suggested in his pseudo-American accent.

Far and Wide

I was expected to have 'an acute awareness' of the institution's welfare programme. I was to be an example of the possibilities for achievement through hard work.

My plan was to move as far as possible from the sweetness of your voice, the springiness of your thigh.

There were bony cows lowing during the night near Singh's Hostel for Foreign Students. The humidity was overpowering and the persistent humming of ceiling fans was an irritating roommate. The sandalwood smell of incense was everywhere.

I thought of you asleep in those satin sheets and I wondered if the cows were lowing in Cumeragh. Were you breathing softly, your chest rising and falling in gentle rhythm? Did you think of me at all Niamh?

In the morning, I manoeuvred through mayhem, dodged motorbikes and the surging of people, lorries and rickshaws. I had read that this city changes people.

I dressed in light black jeans and a white cotton shirt, fearing locals might see me as a moneybag. This proved to be right, beggars everywhere, sitting on urine-washed pavements, well-rehearsed in dealing with first timers. Bearded vendors were touting their wares, massages, hash, boat trips, postcards, silk. You were in my head. I remembered everything, that soft pink of your ears.

After dark, the river came alive, the sounds of horns and bicycle bells, quieter now, giving way to temple music and barking dogs. The cows, drawn to fires lit in lanes, rummaged in plastic bags.

The dog chorus, lacking any harmony, persisted during the night. I wondered if you could hear the farm dogs, perhaps more alert now to protecting you. After all, the man of the house had disappeared.

The first days at The Sunskruti School were challenging; the kids were snotty and condescending. My old skills helped me make an impression.

The 'safe and supportive' learning environment was what one might expect, but the 'up to date facilities' less so. I worked hard but my state of mind was more fragile than that of the spoiled and privileged smiling lot in my care. Autopilot took over for a while.

I learned to sleep in smelting heat. I discovered restaurants which sold what I liked. Pizzeria Ganati. I remembered rainy nights and shared throws. I picked up a few words in Hindi.

मैं ठीक हूँ (main theek hoon)   I am fine.

'I'm fine Tony. Stop bothering me,' you said. Your slight irritation masking more. We weren't fine at all.

The evening I met Miss Taylor was a turning point of sorts. She liked her whiskey and ordered with such confidence at the Sol Haveli I was drawn into her orbit.

'This place is advertised as having great cocktails and best whiskeys. A noisy crowd also it seems.' She appeared to be addressing me.

'Oh don't worry' she went on as if she had read my face. 'I'm not trying to pick you up. Just looking for a chat in my native tongue.'

Her name was Shannon. I thought of the night we rented that little cruiser, Kilkenny 43 all the way to Carrig-on- Shannon, and the sound of your sigh, gentle lapping of the river, as I kissed your soft white neck. I felt your trembling.

We became friends, Shannon and I. She was so different to you Niamh. I didn't always think of you when she came by. There was just that empty space.

Far and Wide

She was Australian, from a place called Nhulunby in the Northern Territory. She called it NT. The thing is, Niamh, she was ill, and the bravest soul I have ever known. Sometimes she confided in me. She cursed her pain and threw things around my apartment. I had rented a flat in Ramrepur by then; one bedroom, one bath, one balcony.

I watched her go through money like there was no tomorrow. We sat in the evenings listening to the hypnotic sounds of worshippers as they buried their dead in the ghats. We drank McDowels.

The whiskey loosened our tongues and didn't mind if we cried. She listened to my agony Niamh. Her pain was all-consuming, but she listened generously, and I was selfish.

'A selfish git,' you often called me and now I realised you were right. About so many things.

We had some fun until her skin became blueish and her breathing ragged. She couldn't eat then and even McDowell was rejected. But she managed to smile as I took her to the hospital. A red sign blazoned with the words 'Infinity Care'.

She got in touch with her family before the end and I went to meet her brother at the railway station. He was angry. But kind when he saw her in the hospital. I left him to it.

Far and Wide

She died in peace; her brother told me. I really don't know what that means anymore. She was cremated and we scattered her in the Ganges as the sounds of India danced on the river.

It was the first time I'd felt something like an affinity with that alien space.

Far and Wide

The Diary

Matt Roberts

The children sat on the wooden floor, crossed legs with fingers on lips. The rain had stopped briefly, giving them a few minutes to make it to school. Their minds raced to the weekend, the games they would play with their friends on the streets of Aberfan. Hopscotch along the narrow terrace, and games of football where jumpers became makeshift goalposts.

It was a weekend just like any other. A weekend that many of the children would never see.

In a single moment the silence was shattered by the resonance of an almighty roar of No 7 tip, a man –made mountain made up of a quarter of a million tonnes of coal waste hurtling down the valley, soon to engulf Pantglas Junior School.

***

Friday 21st October 1966

Written in retrospect 2 weeks later.

Far and Wide

I opened the morning paper, when there came an urgent hammering at my door.

I got to my feet, a moment of resentment clouding my thoughts, annoyed that someone was so forceful with their presence. I opened the door to see Mr Morris from two doors up, his shirt untucked, his hair stood on end. Usually, he was so well put together, a shirt and tie with a Windsor knot, Bryllcreem slickly applied to his hair, but not today. Today he looked as if he had been snatched from his bed and tossed out onto the street. This vision of him so out of sort was enough to convince me that something was wrong.

'Quickly, there's been an explosion or something. Children. Aberfan. Come on.' Words spat from his trembling lips, piercing my consciousness. He turned before I could answer, sure that I would follow. I pulled the door shut and followed Mr Morris to his car.

'What's happened?' I asked, allowing him the time now to relay what he had heard over the wireless only minutes before. Initial reports said that children at a school in Aberfan, just up the valley, were trapped. We would be going to help clear the rubble, to free the children.

How naive we were back then.

How unprepared for what was ahead of us.

Far and Wide

As we arrived, we noticed the road ahead had been closed, undeterred Mr Morris parked on a grass verge and we undertook the rest of the journey on foot. People were out on the streets grim faced, hands rung. Others walked towards us wordlessly, clothes dirty and torn.

We made our way towards the school, the mountain that loomed large behind it showing a trail of destruction, a skid mark strewn downwards. I noticed the collection of miners there before us, they were frantically working at the surface, using their tools to shovel hoards of rocks. I scanned the crowds for tools, a shovel, anything, but I was found wanting.

Villagers had come out in droves, the women had been handing out tools to everyone, but now their reserves were bare. Mr Morris and I descending upon the rubble and joined the effort, rolling up our sleeves and using our bare hands to haul the debris to one side.

It was about twenty past eleven now, and somehow children were still being pulled to safety. These brave souls defied the odds as they clung to their childhood with soot covered hands. They emerged from the rubble, spirit doubled, resilience undoubted. Every single one of them with two requests to their rescuer, the first asking after their mother, the second after a school friend.

Every so often someone would call for silence. A hush would descend over the village as we desperately listened for the cries of those buried beneath us, but our shoulders slumped when the only sound we heard was that of the mother's cries as they sank to their knees.

The only person I ever really spoke to about this, was Mr Morris, we both confessed that it wasn't the bodies that caused us to wake up in the middle of the night. It was the sound of those mothers, the guttural roar that emanated from within them as the sorrow swept over them in crushing waves of realisation.

Thus far, I have never stopped hearing those cries.

Suddenly, my heart leapt and I fell to my knees, scrambling at the rocks, calling for help with a voice that didn't seem to belong to me, so desperate was it. Gently, I eased the body of a small boy out of the rubble as the doctor pushed his way through the crowd.

He knelt beside me, two fingers placed in the crook of a small wrist.

Far and Wide

Around us I could sense the eyes focused upon us, everyone waiting for his verdict.

Bated breath, and whispered prayers to a God we hoped was watching.

The doctor took the little body gently from my arms. He rose to his feet as someone passed him a clean woollen blanket. The doctor made his way over the rubble, head bowed, carrying the child towards a building of corrugated iron which we could only presume was being used as a mortuary.

After this I suddenly felt my feelings overwhelm me, my hands felt alien to me, as heavy as my heart. I crept down the back lane between two terraced houses and slumped against the wall. Sure now that no one could see me, I allowed myself to feel for the first time. I sat and I cried for the first time in many years.

I sobbed until there were no more tears left inside, then got back to my feet, dried my cheeks against my once white shirt, and made my way back to the school.

I had afforded myself the luxury of rest, of feeling, but there was far too much at stake to do that again.

Far and Wide

We carried on like this for hours, we worked until nightfall, until my hands shook from exhaustion. Still, we continued, because when a mother sits clutching her child's cherished stuffed animal, watching you with the last threads of hope in her heart, how can you stop?

Late into the night Mr Morris found me amongst the crowd and told me that he needed to go home. He suggested that we could come back tomorrow, that others would take over in our place, there was no shortage of willing volunteers, people had arrived from far and wide.

At last, our shift was done.

Mr Morris and I had planned to go back the following day, but we convinced ourselves that there were enough volunteers there now that we would not be needed, both of us knowing that in truth we just could not face another day.

It was reported a few days later that 116 children, and 28 adults, had died. Aberfan was a beautiful village, nestled into the hillside, but now my perception has shifted. I no longer see these hills as castle walls protecting us from the world, instead I see them as looming beasts. As a warning that we cannot keep taking from the earth for our own greed, the land that we mine and pilfer took back from us on that Friday morning. Now we have to help heal it before it's too late.

What Lies Within

Miracle Robson

'You don't have much time left,' the doctor closed the folder with finality. 'What are your plans?'

Liz peeled the layers of flesh on her fingers, trying to stop herself from throwing a fit in the doctor's office. She'd been diagnosed with a chronic disease. According to the doctors she had met, there was no exact cause of the disease. They said that she was losing time and her body would finally give up on life.

'Miss Elizabeth?' The doctor's voice cut through her thoughts.

She looked up at the doctor's face with her dark-circled eyes. 'Why do you all say the same thing?' Her voice was surprisingly calm. 'I know I don't have much time left, I don't need a reminder. I am here for a solution not your excuse for a therapy session.'

That last sentence wasn't necessary, Liz reflected. For a second, she bit her lip, silently reprimanding herself for not having more self-control.

Far and Wide

'As you already know, there is no solution. Right now the only choice you have is to live life to the fullest so you have no regrets.'

Liz had to admit that the doctor was either a polite person or a complete snob. So much for doctors being the most compassionate people on the planet.

'Thank you,' Liz smiled although it didn't reach her eyes. She's had it with these doctors. She was going to find a solution. She snatched her brown Berkins bag from the sofa beside her and stood up abruptly. Before she slammed the door shut, she heard the words 'get well soon.' The irony.

***

Gabe sank into the seat of his expensive sofa, a tumbler between his fingertips. He wasn't the drinker kind; he knew well enough what too much alcohol could do to his health. But today, he needed to wash this suppressing feeling away.

He poured more of the Macallan 1926 Valerio Adami into his tumbler before looking around his apartment in pride. He had everything he ever wanted. Everything he dreamt of. Everything… except happiness.

Unlike the popular sayings, happiness had a hefty price tag where he came from. He couldn't figure out the price yet. Sure, his wealth surpassed what he

Far and Wide

imagined, but still, what he really needed was out of reach.

Out of reach. That's it. He has spent money on things he thought would make him happy, but perhaps he needed to think outside the box. He needed to find it.

He opened the door to his walk-in closet. He didn't have the luxury of time to be mesmerised by the quality of the outstanding clothing he possessed. His mind was a nervous wreck, shuffling ideas of places that held his happiness.

He quickly reached for his Keepall Bandoulière that was on the top shelf. He moved his already neatly folded clothes from the drawers into the bag with smooth precision.

***

Paris, the City of Love. Was it really that or was it the city guide's clandestine plot to keep him lurking in the streets of Paris longer than he intended? Sincerely speaking, the idea of love didn't quite sit well in his throat.

He glanced at the pamphlet in his hand, unsure of where his little treasure lay. Ah, the Eiffel Tower. A good place to start treasure hunting.

Far and Wide

He stared for minutes at the Eiffel Tower, unsure if the puddled iron was supposed to throw up a happiness gem from its hinges.

'You might as well climb it,' came a voice behind him.

'Trust me, that is not a bad idea but—' Gabe turned to see someone he'd never thought he'd ever meet again.

'Liz!' Gabe squealed in surprise.

'Gabe!' Liz mocked his demeanor. They were barely acquaintances in high school, although she had to admit that she had missed his personality. She pursued a degree in Medicine at Imperial College, London, while he settled in Texas and ran an empire.

'It's been... four years?' Gabe was obviously shocked; meanwhile, Liz, emotionally drained, felt nothing out of the ordinary.

'Five,' she corrected. She was better at numbers, not that she cared about the length of their years apart.

'So, what brings you to the City of Love?' Gabe asked, needing to start a conversation. A reconnection, probably.

'It would interest you to know that in the 18th and 19th centuries, Paris was the birthplace of modern scientific medicine,' Liz went professor-mode in an instant. 'So, I find it insulting to my medical knowledge to address such a historic place with such… wrong words.'

Liz knew that the words weren't wrong, but she couldn't stand the cliché of finding love in Paris.

As if.

'What brings you here?' She asked.

'Treasure hunting,' he replied with a smile. The Eiffel Tower stood beautiful in the night light but he wasn't happy staring at it.

Liz looked at him awkwardly, fighting back the urge to say something mean. 'Good luck with your treasure hunting,' she smiled and left.

***

Over the weeks, Liz traveled to Paris, South Africa, Germany, Brazil, and India. She had gone for various treatments, drank herbs she only regretted afterward, but everything was still the same.

She was in China, in Jilin, the City of Ginseng. She considered this her last hope, yet she refused to give up. She was walking down the street, heading to an herbal pharmacy when her eyes met Gabe's. She could swear that he had a tracker on her, 'cause why in the whole of China was he in front of her?

Far and Wide

'Hi!' Gabe waved with a childish smile crossing his face.

Liz made a face and walked up to him. 'Why are you here?' Her voice was almost a whisper.

He pointed at the spa behind him. 'For relaxation. I hear it makes people happy.'

Something in his eyes—maybe desire, hope—made her jaw drop slightly. She would be foolish to think that he is following her around when he probably has his own problems.

'You want to be happy?' Liz asked, studying him intently.

He nodded. He had been to places, tried a variety of cuisines, and tried exercising, all of which were great, but he still wasn't happy.

'Happiness isn't out here. It's within you,' Liz said.

'You have to do what you love if you want to be happy,' she continued. 'Not what others define happiness to be.'

Gabe thought for a while before replying. 'I guess I loved playing the piano when I was younger.'

Liz took his hand and raced to a coffee shop that she remembered had a piano. He played Perfect by Ed Sheeran while a female customer sang along. There it was—happiness—swelling inside his heart.

He glanced at Liz who had fallen asleep. He realised that it wasn't only playing the piano, but she also made him happy.

Liz woke up in the passenger seat of a car and was about to scream before she saw Gabe in the driver's seat. She looked at the time and it was 8 p.m. She'd been asleep for seven hours, a rare luxury since she started med school, where she hadn't slept more than two hours. And oh, she felt so good. She wasn't sick after all, she needed rest.

The Great Escape

Anne Silva

As she threw another armful of clothes into her duffel bag, she realised that she never liked any of those clothes. She longed to dress like one of those models in the magazines she saw at Maggie's place. Vibrant colours, bold prints, and a flash of skin. She knew she was beautiful; she saw her face in the bathroom mirror every morning. She longed to wear some red lipstick. She threw the clothes out of the bag. She would buy new clothes.

Next, she wondered if she should pack her government documents. Would she still be herself after today? If the escape were to be an escape, she'd need to be someone else. Not herself. That meant no bank accounts either. She'd have to use cash. She packed the documents anyway, resolving to throw them in a nice warm fire as soon as she could. It wouldn't matter; she never had anything to her name anyway. She didn't even know how to use an atm.

So, she picked up a tote bag instead. It was the bag she took with her when she went to Maggie's house. Maggie had given it to her last Christmas. Of course, he didn't approve of it, but at least he didn't burn it

Far and Wide

like he did with the magazines he found under her side of the mattress.

She filled the tote with all the loose cash she found around the house. She reached for the jewellery and took her hand back. Should she take the jewellery? He made her wear them when he took her to those fancy parties his office would throw. Another shiny object for him to show off. She threw them into her bag. She would sell them.

Her eyes passed over the neatly arranged items in their bedroom. She considered whether any of them would be of any use to her. Grocery lists, planners, an odd fridge magnet that had made its way to the bedroom… a phony smile mocked her from a framed couple photo on the dresser. A dresser with no mirror. He thought a large mirror would encourage vanity in her. Him and his beliefs.

She slipped her feet into the highest heels he allowed her to own. One and a half inches. She walked confidently into the kitchen downstairs with her back straight and her head high. She was already new.

He lay on the ground, his arm reaching towards the cabinet above the sink. He didn't know that she had already flushed down the extra pills he kept there.

His eyes widened when he saw her. He had never seen her look like that. He had not even imagined she could look like that. She looked like she came

Far and Wide

out of one of his dirty fantasies, the fantasies that did not belong in her life, the fantasies that did not come in through the front door of their house.

He gathered all the energy he could to speak a few words. 'You know I need them,' he rasped. 'You know I'll die.'

She didn't reply. She pulled out a chair from the little dining table in the kitchen and sat on it, gracefully placing one leg upon the other. She smiled as if she were at an interview. An interview, a test, that would decide her future. She would make sure that her business at home was completed before she headed out.

His breath was loud and raspy, struggling to hold on to the last few moments of life. But her eyes were set on the road she saw through the bars of her small kitchen window. The road would take her away. Far and wide.

Shay Goodbye

Kerri Simpson

Today, under this roof, there was every variation of our Shay heritage: O'Shay, O'Shee, McShay, O'Sé, and Shea – he's a slippery character. I laughed as I said that last one to my brother - he didn't even snigger - it's not funny if you have to explain it. There was even a traditional Ó Séaghdha, which none of us could pronounce, even Father Ó Séaghdha himself, once he'd had a few whiskeys – and only whiskeys, mind…he wouldn't touch a drop of the *whisky*. He was one of a handful of our relatives who spoke the Irish language, but after the whiskey, it was a tough call which language he was speaking. As long as the barman understood him, that seemed to be the main thing.

I stood in the corner, with my brother, Craig, who took a long swig from a pint of Guinness. He placed his glass on a table beside us and watched it until the liquid settled.

'Like a pro,' he said, proudly, pointing at the position of the foam and liquid. 'Split the G!'

Far and Wide

There was a big cheer from the others in the bar, so he took a bow. I hadn't even realised that anyone had noticed us.

'You Eddie's lads?' asked an older man, holding out a hand that could have shovelled coal, both in size and dirtiness. I hesitated, knowing this wasn't the place to pull a hand sanitizer out of my pocket. Craig went straight in, with a firm handshake, and then rubbed his hands on his trouser legs, without even a bit of embarrassment.

'Yes. Dad couldn't travel but he wanted us to...' I tailed off, not really wanting to repeat what Dad had said. He'd got a bit, outspoken, as he aged.

'Represent the English side of the family,' said Craig, helpfully. He held up an almost empty glass, 'To Uncle Finn!'

There was another universal cheer. Everyone raised their glasses and there was silence, as each was drained. Another barman arrived, as my relatives headed over to the bar, en masse.

'Oh my god! Is that Uncle Darragh?' I asked, pointing to a large man, arm-wrestling a white-haired, elderly woman. 'He wasn't at the Crem.'

Craig peered over my shoulder. 'Nah, Dad said he'd never left the States since he moved over in the seventies. Although...' Squinting, he put on his glasses, presumably for effect, as I knew he'd only

Far and Wide

got them for reading. 'That could be him. A fatter, balder, louder version of Dad. He didn't get the arm-wrestling gene – that lady's beating him!'

'That's no lady,' said the man who'd asked if we were Eddie's sons. 'It's his wife!'

'Auntie Polly!' we said, in unison, in a pitch that caused both her and Uncle Darragh to look over at us. My mind had trouble matching the softly spoken, pearl-wearing woman on our annual Christmas Skype calls, with the tipsy strongwoman.

Uncle Darragh stood up and came to see us, by way of the bar.

'Boys!' he said, patting us on the back so firmly, that my legs buckled. 'Sorry your dad couldn't come, but I see you're representing him.' He nodded his head towards the empty glasses on the table. 'I've had a skinful and Polly's on the Malibu. Maudlin on Malibu.' He shook his head, sadly. 'I'm in for a long night.'

I pulled Uncle Darragh to one side. 'I don't want to sound disrespectful, but does everyone usually get so...*merry*?' I asked, finding the least offensive word that I could, to describe the legless bunch around us, who'd seemingly travelled from far and wide to see Finn off.

Uncle Darragh let out a loud, hearty laugh. 'Didn't your Dad tell you about that skinflint of a brother of

Far and Wide

ours? Wouldn't give you the lint from his pocket. Made Scrooge look like Viv Nicholson!'

The comparison was lost on me but I got the gist. Dad clearly didn't like his eldest brother, from what he'd said, so I wasn't sure why we were here. Uncle Darragh fished a folded card from his suit pocket and read it out to me.

'You are cordially invited to the funeral and Wake of Mr Finn Shay. Family and Friends – *ha, as if he had friends* – to the Kerry Crematorium and afterwards to The Shamrock,' he paused, scanning through the details. 'At the bottom it says, 'The drinks are on me!' and, lads, it's the only time in eighty-two years that he's ever put his hand in his pocket.' He raised his glass once more, 'To Finn, the illusionist. Always disappeared when it was his round!'

Far and Wide

The Road To Nowhere

Sali Andiamo Siyaya

Sanudi Malek woke up to the sound of his alarm. After getting dressed, he brushed his teeth while staring at himself in the cracked mirror.

'It's gonna be a good, good day,' he sang, while spitting into the sink.

Outside, the minibus waited on the veranda, he climbed into the driver's seat, and in no time he was out and into the street.

At the bus station, people were already gathering, and Dyson Pius, his conductor, appeared from the crowd with a wide grin on his face.

'Morning, boss!' he said, slapping the side of the minibus.

'Morning, Dyson,' Sanudi replied with a nod. 'You ready?'

'Always ready.' He said, and he clapped his hands loudly, shouting, 'Town! Town! Town! Let's go!'

People rushed forward. Dyson pulled the sliding door open and began herding them in.

Far and Wide

'Madam, shift inside...eish, don't sit on the edge like that, you'll fall! You too, brother, move to the back, make space!'

The minibus filled up fast, but more people kept coming.

Sanudi frowned. 'This is full,' he said through the open window.

'Dyson, you're not coming,' Sanudi said as he turned around in his seat.

'What? The bus can't go without me!' Dyson said with wide eyes. 'Who will collect the money?'

Sanudi pointed to a lady in the front seat. 'She will pass it back, you stay. We are too full.'

The passengers started complaining, saying that they were late.

Dyson looked at the minibus, then he agreed to stay.

The road to the city was busy, and Sanudi noticed a roadblock ahead, as two traffic police officers stood near it. He knew an overloaded minibus was a sure arrest, or he might be given a fine he couldn't afford.

'Ah, not today,' he said to himself, and turned onto a smaller dirt road on the left he knew well.

Far and Wide

Some passengers wondered before they understood what was happening.

The ride was too smooth, and Sanudi saw trees in both sides of the road now. They were full of dark, round fruits… almost like blackberries, only that they were larger.

These trees weren't here last time, he thought. It was just grass if I remember well, weeks ago.

He heard his passengers complaining that they were hungry and some wanted to relieve themselves.

Sanudi stopped the bus.

'All right,' he said quietly, 'but be quick.'

Everyone climbed out, heading for the trees even Sanudi followed. He plucked one of the fruits, stared at it, as if not sure if he wanted to take a bite or not.

Turning the fruit over slowly in his hand, he felt it pulsing, like there was something alive inside the fruit.

He froze, but it was too late. All around him passengers were biting into the fruits.

Sanudi watched as their ears stretched longer, their eyes widened, their hair withered, and their skin grew scales, and at this time, they were no longer human.

Far and Wide

Seeing this, Sanudi ran to the minibus with the fruit and in no time, he sped off after leaving the fruit on the dashboard. In the rearview mirror, he could see the creatures running after him.

'Not today,' he muttered to himself, and he drove faster, leaving them behind.

He breathed hard, and he noticed something was wrong with the road.

It was so straight. He passed a bent tree on the left, and five minutes later, he saw it again.

'No,' he said. 'This can't be… this road… is going nowhere…'

And then, he froze, before he even finished his sentence.

'Are you going to eat me or not?'

Sanudi turned toward the dashboard.

The fruit… it was talking. Its voice was playful… like it was laughing at him.

Sanudi swallowed hard. 'I…I'm not sure,' he stammered.

'Good answer,' the fruit said, mockingly.

Sanudi tried to hold the question, but he couldn't. 'Where are we? Where have you brought me?'

Far and Wide

The fruit's skin seemed to grow darker. 'This place doesn't exist,' it said softly. 'You drove through a door. Now you're stuck here.'

Sanudi's hands shook on the wheel. 'I just want to go home,' he said.

'Then save them,' the fruit replied. 'Your friends. Turn them back to what they were before the sun goes down. After sunset, they won't come back. They'll stay like that forever and stuck here with you as well, you'll be hunted for food.' And then it laughed, mockingly.

Sanudi stopped the minibus. 'How am I going to save them?'

'Burn the fruits,' the fruit said simply. 'Set them on fire. Throw them at the ones who have turned. When they are all human again and sitting in your minibus, drive through any tree. You will find yourself back on your road home. That's the only way out.'

Sanudi licked his lips, and he was about to ask another question, like how to find fire in this strange place.

But the fruit was gone.

Far and Wide

He turned his head to the back of the minibus and climbed over from the driver's seat. He moved quickly, opening zippers and searching pockets.

'Come on, come on...' he said to himself. 'Somebody must have something... matches... anything.'

One bag had nothing but clothes, and there was nothing useful. He grabbed the last coat and felt something cold and metallic in its pocket.

He pulled it out, and it was a lighter.

'Yes!' He smiled to himself. 'God bless whoever owns this coat!'

He ran to the trees and gathered a pile of fruits. His heart beat louder, knowing that the sun will be going down soon.

He lit the lighter and held it to one of the fruits. To his surprise, it caught fire almost instantly.

Sanudi stepped back, shielding his face as the pile burned hot, crackling as if it had been waiting to be set on fire.

Then he heard rustling noises.

From between the trees, the creatures came. They looked straight at him, and their scaly faces were twisted with hunger.

Far and Wide

Sanudi grabbed one of the burning fruits, and to his relief, it didn't burn him.

He quickly threw it at the nearest creature. The flaming fruit hit its chest, and the creature let out a horrible groan as it turned into human. He grabbed another burning fruit and threw it, then another. The creatures cried and wriggled as they turned back into humans, one by one.

Those who became human again turned to their feet and started helping Sanudi with what he was doing.

After they had all turned to human, they all run to the minibus as fast as they could and the last one slammed the door shut.

Sanudi jumped into the driver's seat and started the engine.

The sky was red now. He pressed the accelerator and drove straight toward the nearest tree… then… they were back. The strange trees were gone. They were on the normal road leading to the city, with cars and bicycles passing as if nothing had happened.

Sanudi just kept driving, it was still day light in his real world and he wondered if whatever had happened to them was a story to tell.

Far and Wide

What Might Unfold

James Tranter

I lean over the sky-ship's rail and look down at the dark jungle, slowly passing by a few thousand feet below. It looks so close through the clouds, I feel like I can reach out and touch it.

The telescope comes to my eye and I start scanning. There's no sign of the ancient Aztec temple!

Legend says it will disappear at sundown. The old bearded man's map seemed clear enough. From Tibet to the Sahara desert, from Hawaii to Peru, this journey has taken us far and wide. Surely we must be there by now.

The telescope comes down. I hear again the wind rushing in my ears. Josephine — my fellow aeronaut — is at the helm near the rear of the sky-ship, squinting into the distance. Her goggles make her eyes look like an insect's.

'Do you see anything yet, Peter?' she calls. I shake my head. This doesn't seem right.

I clamber up to the helm-deck, beside Josephine, and look again between the map and her battered compass. Behind me is the main cabin with only a few paper-thin supplies — and, behind that, the engine-propeller, growling with the effort of maintaining our speed. Bullet-holes from sky-pirate attacks still riddle the cabin and whistle when we go inside. The deck guns are low on ammunition.

Josephine and I both scan. The clouds are bathed in a golden glow from the high sun. The effect is blinding.

I freeze. The sun — my dad always told me that fighter pilots used to hide in the sun. I look up. There's a tiny speck in the sun. Could it be …?

In a matter of seconds, the speck hurtles out of the sun towards us. A fighter! Its wing-guns blaze. I barely have time to think when I run and throw myself onto Josephine. We crash onto the deck. The tracers rake the sky-ship. Wood and splinters leap around us. The fighter flashes by, guns smoking. It's blood-red, with gull wings. "More pirates!" I shout.

There's a deep rumble … Josephine and I jerk our heads up. The rear engine and tail section has leapt into flames. I rush in to the cabin, where swords have now appeared. I grab two.

'Hold on!' she cries as soon as I emerge from the cabin. She grabs the wheel and violently ducks the ship down. I manage to grab the nearest railing to stop myself flying off. The wind howls in my ears. I've lost track of the fighter. The fire around the engine is now roaring like a tiger.

Far and Wide

The fighter comes back into view. It's about 500 metres off to starboard. It has looped around and is matching our dive. Silhouetted against the bright cumulous clouds, it looks like it's floating.

'Look out — he's coming in for more!' Josephine shouts as his nose starts to point again.

I hear two sharp knocks. I snap out of it. Mum has put her head around the bedroom door, catching Josephine and I just as we're ready to fend off another attack.

'Dinner's ready,' she says with a smile.

Hmm ... this was not a good time. But I was hungry, and so was my older sister Josephine. Sky Pirates would have to wait. Hopefully, we'd be back before sundown.

All these memories. I have been silent for a while. Suddenly I am aware of myself, in my childhood bedroom 23 years later, looking into the back of my cupboard: I remember the toilet tubes that were telescopes; the cardboard boxes that made up our sky-ship; the swimming googles that were Josephine's air-goggles, making her look like an insect. It's curious how it brings it all back.

Josephine is downstairs with Mum and Dad, Michael her husband (who is always very chatty),

Far and Wide

and their two children. Maryam, my wife — she's too good for me, a modern-day princess — is with them. I can hear them beneath my window start to scrape chairs and tables on the patio for lunch later.

Further back in the cupboard, I reach and pull out more relics of my childhood: toys, action figures, model cars. Then my old notebooks, full of doodlings: an anti-gravity shuttle with technology from Atlantis … elves and demons in a deadly forest … secret missions behind enemy lines. The products of an imagination roaming far and wide.

When was the last time I wrote a story? I suddenly wonder. It is as if this step back in time has given me a sense of clarity.

The alarm rings on my iPhone (the default "Radar" tone, since you ask). At T minus 15 minutes, the broccoli needs to go on.

At the turn of the stairs is my rucksack. I carry down my childhood notebook, keeping it to myself like I'm a spy smuggling a piece of code. I don't exactly know what I'm doing or why I feel I have to keep it secret. But I feel that I can't let this urge pass me by, so I quickly stick the notebook in the inside pocket — where no one will find it — and close it up.

Mum and Maryam are in the kitchen. Mum still has the warm smile of my childhood. But now her hair is grey instead of black; her face is crinkled instead of smooth. She chatters happily,

'Michael was saying he wanted to know how the IT project was coming along;' I tell her I'll be along in a moment.

I rub Maryam's shoulder and turn the broccoli on to steam. 'How many stories did you write when you were younger?' She looks at me, her warm eyes slightly puzzled.

'You mean, in school?'

'No, just by yourself.'

'I don't remember any.'

Outside, on the patio, Josephine is there, but she's not wearing air-goggles. Instead, she's wearing a wide-brim hat and sunglasses. She's a nurse now; maybe it's the forgotten influence of the time she patched me up after a castle assault. Her children play swords with some sticks in the garden. Dad sips beer and gets some in his old beard. Michael entertains the adults with some witticism he's clearly making up as he goes along, with great confidence.

I have no idea how to write a story, I think to myself. T minus 12 minutes; the chicken will come out soon. *The last dozen things I wrote were project reports, meeting minutes. What will happen if I try?* But, then again, it does strike me that not every kid makes stories in their spare time. The broccoli starts to boil over; I turn the heat down.

The iPhone chimes again. 'Radial', the one for the chicken to come out. But once I silence the alarm, I stare for a moment at the screen. I rush my fingers, click into Notes, open a new one, and write, "I can go far and wide."

It's stupid. I'm making it up as I go along. And now I really need to take the chicken out. I have no idea what might unfold next in the story.

But it's a start.

Far and Wide

Mira's world

Plamen Vasilev

The day Mira left the village, the air was heavy with the scent of rain-soaked earth. She tightened the straps of her weathered satchel, glancing back at the narrow dirt road that wound between rice paddies shimmering under the morning mist. Home. Small, quiet, predictable.

Her grandmother, wrinkled as the bark of the mango tree in the courtyard, had pressed a faded scarf into her hands at dawn.
"Far and wide,' she had whispered, her voice like brittle paper. "That is how dreams must travel. Take ours with you.'

Mira nodded, though her heart quaked. She had never been farther than the weekly market in the next town, but the letter she received—admission to the capital's university—was a rope thrown from the unknown. She gripped it with both hands.

The bus groaned like an old beast as it climbed out of the valley. Mira pressed her forehead to the glass. The landscape slipped past: mud huts shrinking to dots, water buffalo swishing their tails, children

Far and Wide

waving with sticky hands. Her chest hurt with the weight of leaving, but also with the pull of something larger.

She remembered her grandmother's stories of women who never strayed beyond the village, who cooked and birthed and buried until their names faded into dust. Mira was determined not to be one of them. Yet, as the bus lurched forward, she couldn't help but wonder: What if she failed?

The capital was nothing like the village. It was far and wide in every sense—towers slicing the sky, markets bursting with neon, languages colliding in a roar. The air smelled of roasted corn, exhaust fumes, and ambition.

At university, Mira discovered a library so vast she lost herself among its shelves for hours. Books spoke of galaxies, revolutions, and the histories of people who had changed the course of nations. For the first time, she understood how small her village was, how far-reaching her future might be.

But the city was not just wonder. It was also loneliness. Her classmates carried sleek laptops and spoke English with ease. Mira stumbled, her accent thick, her hands calloused from farm work. Nights found her curled in her dorm bed, clutching her grandmother's scarf, whispering the words: *Far and wide.*

Far and Wide

Her chance came in the form of a student competition—an essay on "Bridging Distances.' The winner would receive a scholarship to study abroad. Abroad. The very word sounded like a bird breaking free from a cage.

Mira poured herself into the essay. She wrote of the river that cut through her village, wide and unruly, and of the wooden bridge her people built each year after the floods. She compared it to the invisible rivers—of language, class, geography—that divided human beings, and how knowledge was the bridge that could carry us across.

When she submitted it, her hands shook. Days turned into weeks. Then, one morning, an email appeared: *Congratulations. You are the winner.*

Mira screamed so loudly her roommate dropped her tea. The scholarship was real. She was going farther and wider than anyone in her family had ever imagined.

Her first plane ride was a blur of clouds and silence. She landed in a country where the air was sharp with cold, where trees turned fiery red in autumn. The people walked quickly, their voices clipped and confident. Mira struggled, often lost in translation, but she carried her grandmother's scarf tucked into her coat pocket.

Far and Wide

She studied with ferocity. In lecture halls, she raised her hand even when her voice trembled. In libraries, she devoured books like a starving woman. She learned not only theories and formulas, but also the art of questioning, of speaking up. She was no longer the girl afraid of markets beyond her valley. She was becoming a woman who could stand on any bridge and call across.

Years later, Mira stepped off a bus back into her village. The road was the same, lined with paddies glistening under the sun, but the people greeted her differently. They had heard: she was the one who went far and wide, who studied among strangers, who returned not with riches but with knowledge.

Her grandmother, now frail and bedridden, wept when Mira laid the scarf over her lap.
"You carried it,' she whispered. "You carried us.'

Mira opened a small classroom in the village, teaching children to read, to dream beyond the fields. She told them of galaxies, revolutions, bridges. She told them that their lives, too, could travel far and wide.

As years unfurled, the village changed. Young girls walked with books pressed to their chests. Boys

Far and Wide

spoke of becoming doctors and poets. The classroom grew until it became a school, until it became a beacon.

Mira would sit by the mango tree, watching them run with laughter, remembering the bus ride that had once carried her away. The scarf, faded to threads, lay folded in her desk. She understood now what her grandmother had meant: far and wide was not only about distance. It was about carrying the hopes of many, about letting dreams ripple outward like stones in water.

And so, Mira's name would not fade into dust. It would travel—far and wide.

Far and Wide

32 kilometres

Andrew Walker

The boat looked smaller than Akram had imagined, its fat rubber skin glistening under the moon like a gluttonous seal, gently bobbing on a sea greener than the mined emeralds of Panjshir Valley. Around him, a huddled mass of about twenty asylum seekers muttered in hushed voices, their breath misting the cold air in small clouds. Akram pulled his hood lower as the sharp wind carried a bitter scent of saltwater and diesel. Beside him a woman mumbled prayers under her veil; a man coughed until his ribs rattled; and two boys passed the butt of a cigarette between them.

His memory took him to Lemar's rough, warm hands holding him close in the hidden room above the market. That night they'd smoked charas, laughed, and fucked for hours. They'd eaten sweetbreads topped with honeyed plums and pistachios. Lemar had whispered to him: *Maybe one day we can leave, start again where no one knows us.* Then the door smashed open and they were dragged onto the street, beaten, and humiliated.

The memory was cut off when the boat driver stood before them, cigarette glowing from the corner of his bearded mouth, which he finished and flicked

Far and Wide

into the water, raising his hand to the whispering crowd. His voice came in broken English:

'Listen now. No shouting, no light. You've come from far and wide, yes? Afghanistan, Sudan, Syria... doesn't matter. Now you are same. Same boat, same risk. You move too much, we all go under. You pray to your God, I pray to mine. Maybe morning comes, maybe not. But now - silence. Come, it is time.'

No one spoke. Only the soft sound of the splashing waves and the creak of rubber. Akram stepped forward when his turn came, the sea swirling around his ankles. He climbed into the boat with his carrier bag, clutching a small scarf tucked in his pocket - Lemar's scarf - as the others squeezed in around him, tilting the boat low. Zipping the scarf safely in his pocket, its gentle, masculine scents of caramel, sweet pipe tobacco and peppery oud clung to his hand. Lemar's smell. He buckled a flimsy orange lifejacket onto himself then gripped the side of the boat. The faces around him were lost in cold and fear, as an uncertain future lay 32 kilometers ahead of them.

Shoving the dinghy off the sand with a long pole, the driver started the motor, causing the group to lurch forward as it spluttered weakly to life. As he watched the shore with its industrial skyline slide away like fading, scattered jewels, Akram suddenly longed for the safety of the camp. The night swallowed them, the now black sea stretching into the black sky and beyond like thick tar. For a long while there was only the low hum of the motor, sea slapping the boat, and a few coughs, and then every time someone moved, the boat dipped, the water dangerously close to spilling in. A woman told her child to stay still as someone began to pray in Arabic, his voice trembling, and soon another joined in, then another, until the air was thick with whispered faiths.

Akram stayed silent. His God had abandoned him on that hot morning in the town centre when the square filled with people, and his naked, beaten lover was pushed to the front of them all.

A wave slapped the boat hard, spraying water onto Akram's face, dragging him back to the present. A boy cried out and the driver bellowed for silence. 'Shut mouth! You want coast guard hear? You want police? You panic, we drown!' The boy sobbed silently. Akram closed his eyes and let the sea rock him. For a moment he imagined Lemar's strong arms holding him, whispering comfort, but when he turned there was only an old Sudanese man, teeth missing, eyes squeezed shut.

The boat dipped again, sending water rushing over the sides as it groaned under the weight of too many bodies. Panic spread like wildfire, too many hands grabbing, pushing and pulling, tipping the boat dangerously low, the water now rising fast at the edges. The driver yelled, but his words were

Far and Wide

swallowed by the chaos. 'Calm please! Stay still! Not far now -' He was cut off by a sudden crack from the bottom of the boat. Someone screamed. The woman with a child reached for the rubber sides, but in a heartbeat the child slipped from her arms and was swallowed by the dark sea. Her screaming pierced the black night as she clawed at the edge of the boat, tipping it even further, and Akram felt the weight of it dip, threatening to spill them all into the black sea.

'Don't!' the driver shouted, his face strained. He fought with the pole, trying to stabilize them, but the boat kept rocking. Water sloshed over the sides, now up to their ankles, then their shins. The boat was breaking and it was going to sink, Akram could feel it in the way the rubber creaked and in the way the boat didn't respond to the driver's desperate attempts to steer it. The woman, praying hopelessly for her child, closed her eyes and allowed herself to slip silently from the boat. No one seemed to notice, or care.

Memories of Kabul - Lemar's blindfolded, battered face, his pleading, the podium, the rope - all rocked in Akram's head to the sway of the waves. The sun had burned cruelly that day, scorching the dusty earth. He had fled, like a coward.

Sea water reached their knees now, and then their waists. Akram's heart was pounding. He could hear the others shouting, or was it the crowd baying for

Far and Wide

blood? He hugged the boat tightly as it chugged along despite the water, and closed his eyes for what felt like hours. When he opened them, something appeared on the horizon. At first, Akram thought it was the sea tricking his eyes, but he soon realised that the faint glow was the British shore. The boat was still sinking and they had no way of knowing if they could make it that far. The temptation to let go surged within Akram. The sea was calling for him. He could hear his mother wailing at the doorway, his father's shame. *Leave*, he had said. *You are no son of mine. Don't ever return.*

The water was rising higher now, splashing against his face, the cold sinking deeper into his bones. He could feel the pull of it, the weight of the decision. He could unbuckle his lifejacket and just slip quietly. He could let the black water take him like it had taken the mother to her child. Take him to Lemar and release him from suffocation and guilt. Or he could fight for the shore, for something more than the past. For a future that Lemar could never have.

He whispered a line from the Qur'an - *Indeed, I am near* - and with a final, shuddering breath, Akram made his choice.

Far and Wide

Rider Of The Wild Ocean Winds

Tony Welwig

The sky was blue, the air was cold, the wind was strong, and the Wandering Albatross, from now on named Wanderer, soared over the vastness of the Southern Ocean. Wanderer was a giant of a bird with a wingspan of a few inches under eleven feet and he had ridden the air currents of the Antarctic's Southern Ocean for the past eleven months without ever having touched down on land. Covering a distance of some seventy thousand miles, he had circumnavigated the Antarctic waters in search of fish, squid and other food, and now the draw to return to his birthplace could not be ignored.

Adjacent to Wanderer's remote homeland isle, the ocean waves hummed as they crashed together and bombarded the tall cliffs of the shoreline. Wanderer would never forget this sound for they were unique and were ingrained in his mind from birth. This low-frequency sound was travelling his way from the east, several thousand miles distant, and this was the cue that Wanderer had detected and this was spurring him on.

Soaring in a circle, Wanderer scanned the horizon to the north, east, south and west. From his vantage point sixty feet above the turbulent waves he could see clearly a distance of ten miles. His blue eyes, an attractive and rare peculiarity for such birds, then fastened their gaze to the east upon a dark grey dot that rapidly increased in size. A massive storm cloud was forming and the smell of approaching torrential rain filled Wanderer's nostrils. Adverse weather was coming his way and despite having sensed its approach many hours previously, he had experienced the likeness of such a storm countless times before, and he was confident of riding it safely.

The speed of the wind from the east increased significantly in the space of a few minutes, but Wanderer had now changed direction. His journey home was to be delayed, for turning west would be foolhardy as he didn't want the storm to become a chaser. He chose a northerly direction. Wanderer used the angry currents of air at the storm's edge to soar like a rollercoaster, diving down at an angle with increasing speed, then when near to the water's surface turning upwards using the air energy to lift him ever faster and higher, up and up, forty fifty sixty seventy feet, and to repeat again and again, and continue this inbuilt process that was so instinctive to this wild and intriguing bird.

The sky quickly darkened. Driving rain spattered Wanderer's body only to break up and bounce off his waterproof feathers, then sail away in a multitude of directions. A lightning flash sped down to the ocean surface in a streak of silvery indigo, followed by a clap of thunder that filled the void above the ocean. Wanderer banked involuntarily in a fast angular plunge. He felt the jolt of wingtip upon water and struggled to right himself, and luckily, the upward lift generated by the wind current, lifted his heavyweight body away from trouble.

Wanderer could have sought calm refuge in the eye of the storm, but he knew that by continuing northwards he would eventually rid himself more quickly of the howling wind, gigantic waves, and flying foam. Many hours passed and the long lasting daylight of the south gave rise to encroachment of night time nigritude as he flew into ever lower latitudes. The vivacious ocean had by now become relatively placid, and Wanderer scanned the sky of its stars and moon. He had become disorientated by the fury of the storm and needed time to delve deep into his internal map to effectively navigate back to his island home.

He listened for the humming waves and used the earth's magnetic field, together with the position of the rising sun, to generate an avian compass bearing. Wanderer was now satisfied of his whereabouts. He had a long journey ahead and the yearning for his lifelong partner filled him with increased enthusiasm to complete the journey and meet up with her once again.

Far and Wide

So, the direction was set and Wanderer banked into a semicircular turn to begin flying in a southerly direction from whence he had come when negotiating the storm. A cloudless sky lay ahead and the sunshine seemed to be welcoming Wanderer's pending return after a year at sea. A group of Orcas swam erratically in the blue waters below, chasing various prey, and even though Wanderer hadn't eaten for over three days, he dared not alight on the water to gather the scraps left by the killer whales.

Tiredness began to overwhelm the twenty-seven-year-old Albatross, for lack of food was one reason, but so too was the seemingly endless life at sea without a break on land. Wanderer locked his outstretched wings to save any energy that would otherwise have to be used to hold them firmly in place. He latched onto a tailwind that had suddenly arrived along his flight-path, and with effortless ease he began to soar much faster than before, nearly double the speed.

The long day crept into a short night and then into day again. Wanderer's fast flying was making up for lost time. Distant coastlines appeared on the eastern and western horizons and a cruise ship with waving children nonchalantly went by. The sound of the waves of home grew more pronounced and the smells of home were reaching a high.

On this day in question it was noon in late November and the ocean was bathed in sunshine. A

Far and Wide

short distance from the cliffs of Wanderer's homeland was an anchored fishery ship casting blue coloured fishing lines into the water. Many of Wanderer's brotherhood and sisterhood were floating and swimming amid the deadly mass of baited fishing hooks, for it was that food they were keen to devour. Wanderer was empathetic in knowing that countless numbers of his kind were perishing in the Southern Ocean by becoming caught up, hooked, dragged under and drowned as a result. He reeled away but could never forget.

Wanderer had forgotten his pangs of hunger, for all he wanted now was to be with his partner. The cliff-top became ever-closer and on reaching its edge, he glided in with legs and webbed feet pointing forward, crashing and tumbling to a stop. His webbed feet had failed to act as air brakes. A bit upset by his unruly arrival on terra firma, he looked to his side and was greeted by his mate who had just alighted also. She held a wriggling freshly-caught fish in her bill and deposited it at his feet. Wanderer stared at his partner and a blissfully happy feeling encompassed them both. They circled one another bowing and trumpeting with outstretched wings, then rapidly snapped their bills together. And to strengthen their bond they preened each others feathers, and pointed their bills skyward uttering grunts of pleasure.

Far and Wide

The two avian travellers were together once more after a year of foraging over the hostile oceans, and they will do likewise again and again. Now, they will breed and bring up a chick who hopefully will follow its right to be a rider of the wild ocean winds.

You Ain't Never Had a Freak Like Me

Laura Wise

From far and wide the people came.

They came like the bee to the flower, or the barnacles to the shipwreck, or the leech to the wader's ankle, or the vultures to the corpse.

They came in flocks and flurries. They came from this land and many more beyond.

They came for me.

I was their overpowering flower, their crumbled shipwreck, their grubby ankle and their rotting corpse.

For I was the crown freak of the circus, and they my most devoted audience.

Aha, here they are. Parting the thick, velvet curtain that separates me from the blindingly cheery outside. The Ferris Wheel spinning, the smell of peanuts and burnt sugar, the incessant music and laughter.

That kind of joviality should not be witness to me. It would ruin their carefree fun to be reminded such

Far and Wide

horrors as I live in this world. Occupy space and breath in precious oxygen.

Of course, they all come in eventually. After they're tired of the mindless games and tedious activities, they come in and see something extraordinary and terrible and true.

Men remove top hats from thinning hair, swaggering as their canes clack on the sawdust covered ground. They act as if they're the most important person in the room. But they're not - I am.

As for the women, dressed in heavy drapery, with frilled collars and rib breaking corsets, they emanate a giddy nervousness. They could be heading to the altar, though I doubt they were this excited on their wedding day.

I wonder how that makes the men feel. That a circus freak gets their wives more worked up than they do.

People are craning their necks to see if they can catch a glimpse of me. They will soon but not until its time. Children stuff popcorn into their fat little faces as they hold their parents' hands or sit atop shoulders.

Popcorn. The smell and grease and noise. Hearing these greedy oglers stuff their hands into the red and white striped pot and cram it into their mouths,

Far and Wide

makes me far more nauseous than my own appearance.

I remember the first time I had it. Of course, the first time I tried the buttery nuggets I was utterly infatuated.

He gave it to me. When I was just a boy. A little urchin curled up on the street.

In those days, people ran when they saw me. They averted their eyes and covered their children's. Some even screamed. They still scream, but I think I preferred it when they didn't look. Though, perhaps, I'd miss the attention if it went away.

The day of the popcorn, a man in the most refined dark wool coat and silk cravat approached me.

He didn't run or scream, he stopped and stared.

He crouched down next to me and when I looked up, he smiled. Not with his teeth. He just raised the corners of the mouth that typically dropped downwards. I thought it was friendly then.

A smile of hope and opportunity.

Now, I remember it differently. I remember malice and greed. Of opportunity, yes. But opportunity for him.

Far and Wide

For he had found his shining star. He had found the missing piece of his twisted puzzle.

It was the smile of a spider who'd lured a fly into its web.

He took me to a zoo and there I had the popcorn.

He told me about the circus and said I'd be the crown jewel, the shining star, the pièce de résistance!

He always loved to talk in cliches.

But he entranced me just as the popcorn did. My mind ran away; it hurtled toward the future and the imaginings were utterly irresistible.

I watched people gaze at the tiger in awe and imagined they'd look at me the same way. That those low-lifes who screamed and ran away were insignificant. Once I was with him, on a stage, the main attraction, they would understand. They would know that I was more, that I was the most.

I fingered the flakes and specks of corn and salt at the bottom of the tub, sucking them into that awaiting slit. I bared my tiny fangs and teethed any remaining crumbs from my fingernails.

Far and Wide

He just watched me. That elusive, spider-like smile on his face. He knew he'd caught me. And once *I'd* finished eating, it was time for *his* meal.

Enough of my reminiscence. It's almost time. The audience is sat on the wooden bleachers, hearts pounding. Do they really want to see me? Is it too late to see the elephants instead?

'Ladies and Gentlemen. Boys and Girls. Welcome to the show. A show like none you've ever seen before. A show that will horrify and bewitch. A show you will not easily forget. It'll bury into your minds like a beetle going to feed a carcass to its larvae.'

'I warn you it can be distressing. But something so fantastic and supernaturally strange is worth a little distress. It must be. People from far and wide keep coming.'

'Now without further ado, my cherished audience: I present to you the maimed, the disfigured, the most marvellously horrifying freak in the world!'

'The Man With No Face!'

And then the music plays: 'Doot-doot-doodle-oodle oot doot do do, doot-doot-doodle-oodle oot doot do do.'

Far and Wide

It's called the Entrance of Gladiators. Isn't that ironic? Or maybe it's not. Deep within, I think I've always been a gladiator.

Here I come.

The glass cage is wheeled forward, and my audience sees me, and I hear them.

The gasps always come first. But then there's the screams. Oh, the screams. They fill up my mind and satisfy my soul.

Tell me: what is the attraction of seeing a mangled person? A human who came out all wrong.

It's the unnaturalness, of course but, isn't everyone just fascinatingly grateful they are not me.

But inside they *are* me. They're twisted and grotesque. Whereas I am golden and whole and pure. I am a God compared to them.

Yes. I'm starting to see that now, those tarred insides are fighting their way out…

The screams are coming out different now. Not pure and clean, but oesophagus ripping, ghoulish ones.

I look on and watch as the crowd realises what's happening to them.

Far and Wide

All around the circus, the real freaks are starting to take shape.

Extra limbs are bursting from beneath corsets. Hair is growing over faces and bodies. A calf mangles itself. Nails shoot out from velvet gloves, growing, curling, twisting.

Disgusting.

As I watch them, the golden light within me starts to come to the surface. I can feel myself change too.

Look at me. Beautiful and whole, and worthy of it unlike any of them. A gladiator reborn.

He is looking at me. And I turn to him and smile. The smile of the spider. And it's finally time for my meal.

As for the audience, well now people come from far and wide to see them.

To jeer, to gawk, to point.

And I suppose they will keep coming—until there's no one left but freaks like me.

Far and Wide

Far and Wide

About Croydon Writers

We are a long-established group, meeting regularly each month in Croydon. We also organise one-off meetings and operate a website with helpful information.

Our aim is to offer a supportive space for all writers, young, older, those starting out and the more experienced, to come together to share and develop their writing . All genres are equally valued.

https://croydonwriters.co.uk/

Printed in Dunstable, United Kingdom